BECKA'S AWAKENING

THE WINSTONS SERIES

BOOK I

ROWENA DAWN

SCARLET LEAF

2016

This is a work of fiction.

Names, characters, places and incidents are products of the author's imagination and are not to be construed as real. Any resemblance to actual events, locales, organizations or persons, living or dead, is entirely coincidental.

SCARLET LEAF PUBLISHING HOUSE

TORONTO ONTARIO CANADA

COPYRIGHT BY ROWENA DAWN

ISBN: 9781988397344

For information address:

Scarlet Leaf Publishing House:

scarletleafpublishinghouse@gmail.com

I dedicate this novel to two couples that fell in love at first sight and whose love is always as strong as ever after many, many, many years of marriage:

Dafinka and Giampaolo Scatozza

Diana and Aurel Botorog

Table of Contents

THE WINSTONS

Rebecca's children

    Adam (m. Anna)

    Evelyne (deceased)

Adam's children

    Marjorie (Twin, m. Jonathan) – children: Matt (34), Maggie (28), Jay (28)

    Michael (Twin, m. Amelie) – children: Josh (26), Lily (26)

    Gabriel (m. Emilie) – children: Ariel (32), Alex (32), Becka (19)

PROLOGUE

"Come on, man, this is so not right!" Josh exploded.

He threw his fork back onto the plate and made his aunt, Marjorie, frown. She loved that set of dishes and feared that the young man's frustrations would sooner or later put a crack in them.

"You're complaining, huh?" Maggie waved her fork at him in mockery and rolled her eyes. "You're still fairly young compared to some of us and you have enough time ahead of you, so you shouldn't be the one complaining!" she retorted angrily.

"He has the right to complain, Maggie, as well as any one of us!" Becka replied in support of her cousin. "So what if we are younger? We're all in the same boat!" she punched the table with her little fist. "Auntie, can't we do something about this?"

"I know you want to, pumpkin, but there's nothing you can do about it," Aunt Marjorie stroked her arm in an attempt to soothe her. "What must be done, must be done!"

"So, we have to pay for something that happened a hundred years before we were even born? How does that make any sense at all?" Alex snapped and joined the others in voicing his outrage, though it didn't stop him from scarfing down another piece of pie.

"It's less than a hundred, you nitwit!" Lily replied with disdain and punched his arm.

"Who the hell cares?" Alex retorted with his mouth full.

He never did learn not to talk with his mouth full, try as his parents might. Anyway, he wouldn't have given a rat's ass on such things, anyway, especially at home.

"One hundred, two hundred, same shit, pardon my French. You know what? I don't feel like paying for some jackass's mistakes!" he ended his heated speech, his finger still pointed at Lily.

"So, what do you propose to do, then?" Matt, who had kept his mouth shut until then, asked with nonchalance.

He had been sipping from his glass of whiskey quietly, with a detached expression on his face that suggested that nothing they discussed could affect him.

"Don't tell me you're okay with this!" Alex answered back in disbelief. "Come on, Matt! You're the oldest, man, and you've only got one year left. You've got to be as angry as I am, if not more! Don't pretend it doesn't bother you because that's not possible!"

Matt took a few moments of silence, sipped a little more from his glass, then looked at Alex and shook his head.

"Angry? Maybe. Can I do something about it? I don't think so," he replied to his cousin with his usual coolness, his eyes gazing steadily at him. "So why should I bother?"

No one had anything to say to that. They were all aware there was one stipulation they had to fulfill and only then they could get their trust funds and also reach their full potential.

The worst part was they had to do so before turning thirty-five, because once one of them turned thirty-five without fulfilling that condition, their share of the fund would be divided among the remaining younger ones who still had time to succeed or fail.

"You know what? I don't really care about unlocking my powers," Ariel said pensively, without addressing anyone in particular, "although, it would be nice to see what you can do if you use your full potential..." she continued, lost in her thoughts as always.

Her cousins gave her time to get to the point. They knew she had the bad habit of rambling on and on or getting lost in her own thoughts only to leave everyone hanging. Yet, sometimes, if not most of the time, she could come up with some very interesting solutions if they had the patience to listen to her.

"But I do care about doing something for myself. I'd like to open a little business..." Ariel finally said longingly.

"Keep dreaming, girl," Maggie snapped, already bored with the way Ariel always liked to drag things out. She wasn't one for patience and, unfortunately, that trait had had some unpleasant results in her daily life. "Till you take care of your part of business, Ariel, girl, you won't be able to open a shed."

"Why are you always so mean to her?" Alex snapped at Maggie. "If she wants to dream, let her dream away. What else can she do? What else is there for any of us?" he asked, his infuriated gaze scanning each one of them to see their reactions.

"Beat the curse?" Marjorie asked softly, trying to defuse a potentially explosive situation.

"Not so easy, auntie," Ariel said sorrowfully. "I tried, you know... Do you remember? I thought that guy, Eric, the one I met two years ago, would be the one. It wasn't meant to be, you know... It's not so easy, and you know it very well. You see how things are. There's no real romance left in this world, I'm afraid. If there's no romance left, where can one find true love?"

Marjorie nodded. She did know it. Finding true love wasn't easy-peasy. She'd been in the same situation when it was her turn and she'd almost lost everything because of her own stubbornness and her family's meddling.

"It's never easy, my dear, I know," she answered and stroked the young woman's arm with love again. "But, Ariel, sweetheart, you have to keep trying. You can't simply give up. Think about it! You will be able to use your powers and get your money, but only once you find your true love and commit to it. You'll be truly happy then!"

Ariel turned her eyes to her plate on the table. She knew her eyes would show everyone she'd already resigned herself and she was sick of hearing platitudes and encouragements whenever her family got wind of something like that.

Everybody around the table remained silent for a few moments. Jay helped himself to some more of his mother's amazing pie.

Marjorie was the best cook in their family, which was why they always chose to meet at her house. Everything was easier to swallow if there was a good pie or cake on the table. At least, in Jay's opinion.

"I think we should see if there's any legal way to get out of this situation, guys. We need the money now, don't we? It's not like we can wait around forever!" Alex broke the silence, when the idea came to him suddenly. His eyes analyzed them carefully and saw them nod their assent. "Look," he continued, "I'm already thirty-two. I don't have time for stupid things and games and all sorts of idiotic attempts at love! I want to do something for myself like Ariel said. Now, while I still can."

Although almost everybody found themselves in agreement with him, they still looked at Matt. He was known to be the smartest guy in the family and they knew that any kind of solution should have come from him. Matt's eyes shifted around the table, feeling their expecting gazes on him and finally shook his head.

"There's no way out, buddy," Matt put his glass on the wooden table at the same time and stood from the bench. "If you called us here just for this discussion, then I'm out of here. I've got real things to do, places to see…"

"You don't even want to try," Becka cried out, jumping out of her seat. "You've just given up because you have so little time left and you don't care anymore."

"I tried, sweetie," Matt told her with a sad smile on his lips.

Becka was his favorite cousin. Maybe because she was the youngest or maybe because she was unspoiled and funny and had a very big heart. His fingers stroked her cheek in a loving, yet sad caress, and he kissed her forehead.

"Becka, I tried hard to find any kind of loophole in the wording of the trust funds papers. Believe me, there's none. If I couldn't find one, sweetie, then no one can, and you know it. There's a reason I'm one of the best attorneys in the country, and all of you know this isn't just my vanity talking. Anyway, honey, these days, I content myself with making my own money the hard way and enjoying as much as possible the little spare time I have left. I've stopped chasing such dreams. It's not in the cards for me and that's it."

All of his cousins looked at him in shock. Only his sister, Maggie, understood him very well. She didn't have any patience, especially with fools, but Matt was something special.

She'd always looked up to him and she knew he wasn't the kind of guy to give up on anything without a fight. Hearing him say he'd resigned himself made her understand the depth of his anger, even though he hid it from them.

She felt like taking him into her arms and never letting go but she knew he wouldn't like that. He wasn't very big on displays of affection, her brother, so she just lightly petted his hand and left it at that.

"Matt, you should try to use that time you have left to find a girl," his mother said reproachfully and everyone's attention turned to Marjorie, who continued, "You still have a chance, son, and I'm not talking about the money here, you know it. I know that sad affair with Velma's left you afraid to commit again and I don't like that in the least. That's not the Matty I know. That wasn't love, son, and you know it. Had it been true love, you'd have had your full powers by now even if you hadn't gotten the money."

"Mother, Velma's been out of the picture for a decade already. She's in the past. What's the point in bringing her back into the conversation?" Matt retorted curtly, shaking his head. He couldn't understand his mother's reasons for bringing up bitter memories.

"Because she was the reason you stopped looking at women with hope," Marjorie pointed out, shaking a scolding finger at her first born. "You think all women are like her and that's why you just take everything you can from them and move on. Another woman on the list! It's like you're keeping a score: how many women can Matt score?" she reproached acidly, which wasn't something that they'd witnessed before. Everyone's eyes were riveted on her. "It's not good for you, Matt! Even if you've already given up on the trust fund, which is stupid, by the way, you're still alive and you still need a reliable woman in your life, like I've already said over and over again. You'll grow old and alone and bitter!" Marjorie ended her unusual tirade by punching her son's chest with her finger.

"Thanks for the heads up, mom. It's always good to know what your future will look like!" Matt replied sarcastically and removed himself from the path of her pointy finger. Yet, he didn't leave. He seemed undecided and glance back at his cousins.

Marjorie shook her head bitterly, but chose not to continue that line of discussion. She knew her son quite well and she knew there was no way to make him change his mind when he was like that. It was like talking to a rock.

The silence stretched for a few minutes. Everyone was busy either eating their pie or playing with their drinks, pretending nothing out of ordinary had happened between Marjorie and her eldest son. But mostly, they were busy avoiding each other's eyes for fear someone might say something hurtful again.

In the end, Alex, the most outspoken of all, couldn't stand the awkward silence anymore and looked around the table, gauging everyone's mood. Uncertain whether it was even worth it, he shrugged and decided to try a new line of conversation.

"You know, you are the old lady's favorite great-grandson, Matt. Can't you persuade her to end this foolishness? She can change the papers if she wants to. It's not like the words are carved in stone!" Alex anxiously waited for his answer.

"Tried that too, Alex." Matt sighed, shaking his head. "She said she did it for our own good, whatever she means by that. So… I can say I've tried everything and it's time to limit my losses."

Again, no one said anything for a few moments and, again, they couldn't bring themselves to look each other in the eye and the silence stretched on.

Encouraged by the unusual silence, since such get-togethers were normally a very chatty and loud affair, Matt took his leave with a simple wave of his hand and started down the path to the kitchen door, whistling softly to himself.

Ariel, pensive as always, looked after him until he was out of earshot, and said dolefully, "It's sad… It's really sad. He's the oldest and he's already given up."

For a few moments, everyone stared at her absolutely speechless. It was like she'd grown a second head during the last hour.

"Well, we're close to that too, Ariel," her brother Alex retorted angrily after a moment of disbelief. "It's not like we have too much time left, is it? Just about three years, you dimwit! Once we turn thirty-five, everything will be gone: the money, the powers, everything. And we can't do a single thing to stop this!"

"We can't even cheat," Jay intervened bitterly for the first time and the others burst into laughter.

"Oh, yeah, I remember," Lily said. "You tried to pose as a fool in love and came with that simpleton. Camilla, I think her name was?"

Jay nodded smiling. He had already forgotten the ridicule he'd suffered at the time. His easy-going nature didn't allow him to keep a grudge for long.

"Yeah, but it didn't work, did it?" Josh said very matter-of-factly. "Those two fossils sniffed you out."

"Well, they can read minds, so it was a piece of cake to sniff him out," Aunt Marjorie pointed out with an enigmatic smile on her lips. "That's why they've been appointed trustees, you know. No one can fool them. You shouldn't have tried to cheat, Jay. The old lady hasn't forgiven you for that yet."

Jay shrugged. He knew very well where he stood with his grandma those days. He didn't think she would ever forgive him.

The old bat was a real piece of work. She was resentful and bitter.

Just a few of them could steal a smile from her and lately he hadn't been part of that group. After the stunt he had pulled with that woman, grandma didn't even acknowledge him at the family dinners anymore. She pretended he didn't even exist.

He looked around and noticed all the others had gone quiet, each of them thinking about the implications of what had happened to him.

He truly hoped he wouldn't go through a new period of veiled mean jokes or even innocent teasing. At which Becka was a master. He even flinched when she started speaking, expecting the worst.

"So, we only have to wait for them to die..." Becka tentatively began to say, her gaze passing from one to the other.

"Not so fast," Marjorie interrupted her hastily. "The rule says that if they pass away, two others will take their place. Same type of power, pumpkin, so no way to fool them either. You have to understand there is no way around this. You have to play by the rules."

"Damn it!" Alex swore. "All this drama only because great-grandpa had the nerve to abandon great-grandma for another woman and then another idiot left aunt Evelyn at the altar and she killed herself!" he shook his head as if everything was inconceivable for him. "So, now, generation after generation has to pay for those two idiots! Where the hell is the justice in that?"

"Well, I think it was a radical conclusion from my grandmother, as well," Marjorie replied conciliatorily, "but there's never been a way to change grandma's mind, unfortunately. I know my father tried hard at the time, but she wouldn't listen to him. He tried again when my happiness was at stake and still nothing. He didn't have any success. She wouldn't give in. Not even a bit.

Since the money was still hers, she had the right to decide what she wanted to do with it."

"But why the curse on our powers? I really don't understand that," Becka wondered.

"Same reason. Grandpa was a witch himself and he used those powers to entice a very young woman and leave grandma. And the man who left Evelyn at the altar was also enticed by a witch. She didn't want any other witch to misuse their powers."

"I wouldn't!" Becka cried out.

"I know you wouldn't, pumpkin," Marjorie patted her hand tenderly. "Not all apples are rotten, I know that much. But grandma didn't want to hear a thing, so… Here we are: now, everyone in my generation paid for that and yours has to pay, as well. However, if you succeed in finding your true love and get your trust funds, then at least the money problem will end and the next generations will have only the curse to defeat," Marjorie tried to lift their moods, but with little success.

"Oh, just that," Lily sighed and put her chin in her hand, fixing her dreamy gaze somewhere in the distance.

"I really wanted to open that nursery," Ariel whispered inconsolably and her brother stroked her fingers, his eyes shining with deep concern for his sister's dreams.

"Nothing is lost, sweetheart," Marjorie said and stroked Ariel's hand at her turn. "You'll see. You'll find your soul mate, Ariel. Everything will be fine."

"Where? Where could I find my soul mate, auntie? The people I deal with every day are not even lover material, believe me. I wouldn't let them touch me with a ten-foot pole, so finding a soul mate is quite out of question. There's no chance for me out there! I've looked around for years and nothing!" she said, this time with tears in her eyes.

"Wait and see, Ariel. These things have a way of working out," Marjorie whispered to her, then started picking up their plates to show them that the conversation ended.

There was no point in debating something they couldn't fix. There wasn't anything more to add and whining wouldn't help. The older woman knew it well. Whining never helped. You had to roll up your sleeves and do something.

Although the others jumped out of their seats to help her, they were all still thinking about the conversation and a none-too-rosy future, which looked pretty hopeless for them at that very moment.

CHAPTER ONE

Becka left the coffee shop in a hurry. She was holding a hot coffee cup in one hand, while, at the same time, she was trying to stick a muffin and a toasted bagel in her handbag with the other.

She'd forgotten to ask for a hot sleeve for the cup and on top of that, she'd also forgotten to take a napkin. Her head was deep in the clouds that morning, and now, the searing heat burned her fingers through the paper cup.

She couldn't go back to the coffee shop. She was already late for her morning classes and the last thing she wanted was to miss the entire lecture on her favorite subject.

Becka kept struggling. She tried to make the muffin and bagel fit in her handbag, at which point she wondered why she'd left the house with such a tiny purse.

The people and things around her became a blur the more she wrestled with the bag and the more she rushed toward the bus stop.

No more than a moment later, just as she turned around the corner, her eyes still on the tiny handbag that wouldn't cooperate with her, she ran into a tall man and as luck would have it, the lid of the coffee cup came loose and all the hot liquid spilled all over the giant's pristine, white shirt.

Of course, Becka thought, things couldn't get any worse! Not only did she scald him but the damn shirt had to be white! Why not black? No one would notice a coffee stain on a black shirt!

"Oh, my God, I'm so sorry! Really, really, sorry!" she blabbered and tried to clean his shirt with her bare hands, forgetting about the cup lying on the pavement, discarded like yesterday's news, all but empty. She'd also forgotten about her coveted breakfast, which was leaning precariously on one side of the handbag, ready to fall out as well.

Her hands shook the man's shirt as fast as she possibly could. Her meager attempts hoped to limit the burns at the very least.

Becka knew the hot coffee must have already penetrated his shirt and she didn't even want to think of what had happened to the skin beneath it, badly burnt by the freshly boiled brew.

"I think you'd better take your shirt off!" she cried out, without taking her gaze off the task at hand.

Remorse drove her actions. Images of the emergency room flashed at the back of her mind. Focused to a frenzy on her nearly catastrophic mistake, Becka never noticed the rest of the man to whom the chest belonged, much less the eyebrow which shot up as soon as she ordered him to strip.

"May I ask what exactly you're trying to do?" he finally asked in a deceptively mild tone.

Until then, he'd simply looked at the top of her head, completely shocked by the actions of the little woman before him.

Hearing his voice, she finally looked up and blinked. Not once or twice, but three times. The man she had in front of her wasn't the regular polished and polite man she'd encountered in her life before. He was a far, far cry from that.

This man's rugged face was set off by a long, pale scar on his left cheek that began somewhere close to the corner of his eye and continued to nearly the corner of his mouth, giving him a dangerous allure. He looked like one of the mercenaries she had seen in one of the documentaries about the civil war in former Yugoslavia. It wasn't reassuring.

His eyebrow was still raised scornfully and for a moment there, she asked herself how he did it. It wasn't easy to pull off that move for so long, she imagined. The young woman just about forgot her curiosity when she met his eyes, colder than the Arctic Ocean. She almost shivered.

She blinked again, swallowed hard and tried to find her voice. She forced herself to be brave, refusing to even consider the thought of being a scaredy-cat. She'd always tried to face any danger, not run away from it, and that wasn't the moment to change her ways.

"Hmm…. I was thinking… you know… your shirt…"

"I heard that bit about my shirt, don't you worry, but I really don't know what difference you think it would make if I took it off now. With or without the shirt, my skin is still scalded, my morning's still ruined and I'm still pissed off..." he said in a level tone, which didn't show the slightest hint of anger and that made her even more fearful.

While it was true he didn't sound mad, the complete clash between his words and his tone made her nervous. Becka couldn't even begin to think of how to talk to him.

She swallowed again and bravely said, "Yes, I know that, but the coffee is mostly on the shirt, so if you take it off..."

"Now?" he mused, when he saw she stopped without finishing her sentence.

"Well, yes," she nodded and stressed her words, in an effort to lend them more confidence than she had.

She pretended she knew what she was doing, although her face was burning in absolute embarrassment and shame.

It was the first time she'd ever asked a man to take his clothes off, even though it was only the shirt. On top of all that, his tone and attitude made her terribly uncomfortable and she was afraid that everything showed on her face.

She couldn't say she had a poker face worth a damn. Every time she played cards with Jay, he would laugh at her best, yet failed efforts to bluff.

The man looked at her for a few seconds, but then, with a bold move, he took his shirt off.

"Do your worst!" he said and handed her the all but ruined piece of clothing.

However, Becka didn't take it. She didn't even notice he was holding anything for her to take. She couldn't even find her voice to answer back. Her eyes were too busy taking in the expanse of a chiseled chest peppered with curly coarse hair, still wet from her coffee. She'd forgotten what she wanted or was supposed to do entirely.

"Earth to the moon?" he mocked her in his grave voice and waved his hand before her eyes.

Finally, his gestures pulled her out of her reverie and Becka's eyes shot up to meet his in an instant.

"Sorry, just lost in thought for a moment there," she mumbled more than a little disappointed with her silly admiration of the male figure. She'd thought herself above such trivial endeavours.

Finally, she took the shirt from his waiting hand and used it to dry his chest more vigorously than it was necessary.

The coffee was already a dry sticky stain, but that wasn't on her mind and neither was the fact that she might take off a layer of vulnerable, burned skin, too.

None of those things dawned on her because, to be truthful, Becka was brimming with embarrassment, upset with herself for her carelessness and every reaction that followed.

Not only had she poured her coffee all over a stranger but she'd been caught staring at the man's chest like a lustful, simple-minded woman.

"Yeah, I noticed," he replied amused, watching her expression while she cleaned his chest.

The man enjoyed her train of thought. He could read it on her face with no effort whatsoever.

It was refreshing to see someone so unspoiled like the woman before his eyes. He was tired of all the games played in society and wanted something new.

After a few moments, he decided to ask, "Does any man's chest have this effect on you or just mine?"

There was a little malice in his voice and that made her straighten up and look directly into his eyes. Then, she replied sulkily, "I'm just trying to help, you know! Why are you acting like a jerk?"

When she snapped at him, his eyes became colder than they had been before and he yanked the shirt out of her hands.

"Yeah, with such help I wouldn't be surprised if I'm dead tomorrow!"

She tapped her foot in frustration, raised her voice a notch, and replied to him with her usual self-confidence, "You're just pissed off because I ruined your shirt."

Her voice mustered all the determination she could and she added a nod, for good measure, in the hopes it would give her more of a knowledgeable air.

"But it was just an accident, you have to understand. It wasn't like I wanted to spill my coffee all over you! I'd have preferred to drink it, you know," she scoffed and shrugged her shoulders.

She was standing tall before him, matching his confident, dominant attitude with her own, but spoiled everything when she continued in the tone of a stubborn and willful child, "I really could have used that coffee!"

Fascinated with the sudden change in her attitude, he looked at her more attentively. Only now, he noticed her chocolate eyes and especially her little mouth, arched like a bow, with rosy lips. A part of him was almost begging and pushed him to grab her already and just have a taste of her sweet, sensual mouth.

The longer she talked, his interest in her lips only grew more and he got to the point of an agonizing need urging him to lean in and claim what he wanted. He found them more tempting when the tip of her tongue came out and nervously licked her upper lip. Something stirred inside him and, suddenly, his interest changed completely.

"You owe me," he said so abruptly that it charged the atmosphere in an instant.

Becka opened her mouth in shock to reply. Yet, she couldn't make a sound for a few moments. She was too stunned by his sudden outburst.

The man didn't clarify his statement or expand on it. He just waited for her to process his words and get back to him with a bold retort. From what he'd seen so far, he was sure to get one. He didn't have to wait for too long.

"What are you talking about?" she finally managed to say, with a touch of thinly veiled indignation, and her wide eyes held his own intently.

"What you heard," he brushed off her harmless furor and continued, "You owe me."

"For this shirt?" she asked incredulously, showing him the shirt she held in her hand.

"Among other things."

His wolfish smile ran shivers down her spine, as her mind started dreading the worst and conjured unsettling scenarios.

"What other things?" Becka asked, although more than a little hesitation and uncertainty delayed her question.

Her eyes seemed to grow wider still and the tip of her tongue again touched her upper lip nervously, to torment him and make him more aware of his increasing desire for her.

He couldn't understand that irrational, unlikely desire for a clumsy woman he'd just laid eyes on, but something in him wanted her. He actually needed to have her, just like that.

She looked a bit young, maybe too young, that was true enough, but he knew that looks were sometimes deceptive. He still made a mental note to ask her about her age. He didn't want to fool around with jailbait even though he was agonizingly drawn to her.

He had a strict policy about going to jail. His policy was simple enough. Jail wasn't a place he ever yearned to see on the inside. He did once and even once in a lifetime was more than enough.

"You scalded me, ruined my shirt, and obviously, I can't go to my appointment half-naked. And, please, note, it's an important appointment, and I'm already late because of you," he explained patiently, as if he'd been talking to a small child.

Of course, it was all just a ruse. He was only trying to see what kind of reaction he could draw from her.

She felt the blood rush to her face and she cursed her pale complexion that revealed too much and in the most inappropriate of moments.

No matter how much she tried to appear sophisticated or cool-tempered, she always failed because her skin betrayed her. It was the curse of her life. Maybe not the only curse she had to contend with but it made the top three.

Becka thought of going a different way with him, to get herself out of the trouble that seemed to be brewing, and, very politely, said, "I'm very sorry for scalding you and for ruining your shirt. Of course, I'm sorry about your appointment as well, but I don't see how I could..."

She never finished her sentence because she saw a naughty smile flourish on his lips. That made her lose her train of thought again. This time she was afraid of what he'd say.

"I think you owe me something and you can set it right by going on a date with me," he finally specified his conditions in a tone implying too many things that would better remain unsaid.

"A date with you." she repeated automatically as if she weren't able to grasp the concept.

"Yes, princess, a date," he repeated in a tone that showed he meant it. "You know, that thing where we go somewhere, have something to eat, talk, that sort of stuff. It's usually called a date. So, that's what I want. A date with you... Today. Not right this moment because I obviously can't go anywhere without a shirt, but right after you go into that store over there and buy me another shirt. Don't worry about it, though, I won't ask you to pay for it. I'll give you the money," he waved his hand magnanimously, as if the price of the shirt had been the problem.

"That won't be an issue. I'm the reason you need a new shirt, so I can buy it," Becka replied, offended by his condescending attitude.

"No need," he dismissed her concern, took his wallet out of his back pocket, and pulled a few bills out.

"Here, that should be enough," he said giving her the money. "Now, go in, buy me a white shirt – keep in mind, white shirt, not blue, not black or green, or striped or whatever. Just white. Then we can go on our date."

"No, I can't," she said stubbornly, with a shake of her head.

"Why not?" he asked, his face so rigid and serious as if it had been set in stone. He didn't seem to take her rejection too well. "As I said, you owe me. I can say you attacked me, you know."

"Ha, good try!" she scoffed at him. "Attack by coffee! A deadly weapon! Don't make me laugh. No one would believe that stupid thing and you know it full well. Everyone will see it was a simple accident and nothing more."

"So then, am I to understand you're too good for the likes of me?" he frowned.

Becka scoffed again, and dismissed his silly, inconsequential words with a wave of her hand.

"Get serious! I haven't even considered that. But since I don't know a stitch about you or your life, it would be difficult to make such assumptions, don't you think?"

"Is it my scar?" he asked peevishly now. "Do 'stiches' make you uncomfortable?"

She scoffed at him again, but refused to answer a question she thought to be quite stupid and not worthy of her attention.

"You're not legal, is that it?" he tried again, determined to get her to admit to something.

He didn't understand why but he couldn't just let go.

"No, I am legal enough. I'm not jailbait, don't you worry about that. Three months over nineteen already," she replied, this time smiling warmly at him, which puzzled him a little more than her former, vague refusals.

"So? You have a boyfriend, then, and you won't cheat on him," he tried again.

He'd already reached the point where he just wanted to find out the reason, end the conversation and walk away if she kept rejecting him. He had no explanation for that, but finding out why she wouldn't go out with him was still a priority.

"No, I don't have a boyfriend. However, I do have a class right now and more later on. The point is I really don't want to miss any of them and I'm already so very late... But, if you still want to, I can see you in the afternoon..." she said and saw he was astonished that she actually agreed to go out with him. "And not because I owe you or anything stupid like that, but because I'd like to see you again. I don't owe you a thing! Just so we're clear!"

His eyes searched her face thoroughly. He wanted to make sure she wasn't trying to string him along, but brushed it off after a second of thought. He was almost certain she wouldn't show up, but he didn't have anything to lose, nor could he force her to date him. Anyone would have laughed at him if he'd pretended he was attacked by a girl with a Styrofoam cup of coffee.

"All right," he accepted. "When?"

"If you want it to be today, then it will have to be after four," Becka answered cheerfully, visibly keen on the unexpected date.

"Dinner, at six?" he asked her.

"Why not? I do need to eat dinner."

"This spot here, where we are now?" he asked again.

She nodded, a little amused by his way of asking questions, and turned to leave.

"Hey, you forgot my shirt!" he cried out after her.

"I'm buying it now," she turned her head back to him.

"Take the money, then," he insisted, stretching his hand out to her. "I don't want you to pay for it."

She was stubborn enough to go against his wishes. She did want to have it her way and leave him with his hand outstretched, but took note of the dogged expression on his face and realized he wouldn't give up so easily. He was much more wilful than she was. She gave in and took his money.

CHAPTER TWO

The man paced back and forth impatiently on the corner of the street. In the beginning, when he got there, about five minutes earlier, he'd decided to wait patiently, although he was almost sure she wouldn't show up. He was convinced she had used her classes as an excuse just so she wouldn't have to go on a date with him at all.

The young woman seemed delicate and sheltered. That led him to believe she would avoid any further contact with him.

He had seen that type of woman before, those sheltered flowers, living in a polite world, where everything was covered under several layers of paint to deflect reality. Well, in his experience those innocent flowers would run away like scared rabbits once they took a good look at him and his scar. None ever stuck around for a second chance.

He didn't harbour any illusions about romance or anything of the sort. That was some baggage he'd left aside sometime in his past. He was aware he wasn't the type of man about whom a girl like her would ever dream. He didn't fit the mould of a man she would bring back home to meet mom and dad.

Thank God, he didn't have such aspirations! He was too much of a realist for something like that and even though he didn't want to admit it, he was too terrified to put himself out there in the open, to reveal what was in his soul. It wouldn't have been a smart move. Someone would certainly stomp on it.

He glanced at his watch as he continued pacing around and was surprised to see that he'd actually arrived too early for their meeting. There were about three minutes left until six and he knew he would wait, not only until six o'clock, but probably even ten or fifteen minutes past six, even though he didn't expect her to keep her promise.

Somewhere, at the back of his mind, there was the knowledge he'd partly set up that date with her only to punish himself. He was very good at teaching himself over and over again not to reach for someone as innocent and wholesome as the girl from that morning.

He'd been warned against such wishful thinking many times in the past, but he still found a sort of masochistic enjoyment in challenging fate as if his turn would certainly come one day and then he would win for once. He liked beating the odds.

He was striding on the sidewalk nervously when, suddenly, he saw her rushing towards him. She was pushing past the moving crowd in a hurry, much like she had that morning.

It occurred to him that, probably, being late was one of her habits. It wasn't the worst habit in the world, anyway. He'd seen worse things than that. This was one bad habit he could live with.

This time, at a second, more appraising, glance, the first thing he noticed was her honey-colored hair flowing over her shoulders, thick and full of curls. In the morning, she had it gathered in a thick ponytail. He'd liked her hair that way too. That mass of hair was too rich and vibrant not to like it. However, right then, with that wild mane set free, the young woman was much more enticing than he remembered.

A slow smile flourished on his lips and he wasn't even aware he was smiling, although such an endeavour was something out of the ordinary for him. The longer he watched and admired her, the more he realized he could fall for that girl and in a bad way. The thought troubled him enough and made him frown for a second, erasing any trace of his earlier smile.

The young woman stopped abruptly a few steps away from him and smiled shyly. Her smile reached her eyes and colored the chocolate of her iris in a warmer nuance than the one he'd relished so much just hours before. In that very moment, he was sure he would give her anything she wanted just to enjoy her sweet eyes a little more.

"Hi!" she was out of breath by the time she reached him and her lips arched a little more, tentatively. "I'm really sorry I'm late but I had a bit of a problem at home and I had to take care of that. That's why I couldn't leave earlier. My kitchen flooded. Again."

"You're not late, it's okay. It looks like you're not having a very good day today, though," he replied with a smile, amused with the way she talked.

Her voice had a lower pitch than the voice of some of the women he'd dated and he appreciated it didn't chime like tiny bells in his ears every single time she opened her mouth. He hated the high pitch of an all too sweet, dishonest voice.

"I think we should introduce ourselves for the beginning. I'm Bryan, by the way," he said and his uncharacteristic smile lasted surprisingly long that time.

"Becka," she extended her hand to him enthusiastically, which made his smile grow wider.

She didn't seem reluctant at all to go out with him and that got his hopes up. His perpetual smile hinted at his changing expectations and opinion of her.

"Hello, there, Becka. Nice to meet you." He took the narrow hand in his and shook it lightly. "So, aside from nearly sending a complete stranger to the hospital this morning and the flood this afternoon, how was your day?" he continued, and turned her towards the strip of shops without letting her hand go.

"Well, I was too late for my first class this morning, which annoyed me. Immensely." She rolled her eyes in frustration, as she fell into step with him. "I really like that class, you know. Worse, now, I'll have to figure out everything I missed by myself, which means a lot of work and at least an entire afternoon wasted," she complained.

"So now you resent me," he replied in a low and flat tone.

"Why would you say that?" Becka turned to him surprised at his strange reaction. "I was late even before I bumped into you. It's not your fault at all. It's just I didn't sleep much last night, too many thoughts, you know how it is, and this morning I had a bit of a slow start to my day, that's all."

He nodded once. He understood she didn't blame him or begrudge him for it, but he was more content because she still let him hold her hand than anything else.

"What kind of thoughts could keep a young girl like you awake?"

She scowled at him because of his condescending tone and said peevishly, as she turned her nose up, "The kind of thoughts I can't share with you."

"Hmm," Bryan mumbled but let the subject drop once he saw she was determined not to say anything. He didn't want to push his way in too abruptly and scare her away too soon.

"By the way, I know an Italian restaurant by the lake", Bryan told Becka, squeezing her fingers. "They have a nice terrace overlooking the lake, a gorgeous view … Not to mention, they serve original Italian food. I've heard it's an unforgettable experience."

"I'd love it!" She looked up at him and a wide smile appeared on her lips. "But are you sure we can get a table at this hour? If the view and the food are so great, wouldn't it be packed now?" Becka worried.

"Don't worry, sweetie," he waved her concern off. "I've already made reservations for us."

"So, you were very sure on you… or rather on me… You were sure I'd come…," she murmured to herself, but Bryan heard her anyway.

"No, not at all," he contradicted her. "Actually, I didn't even think you'd show up, but I'd have gone out for dinner anyway so…"

"Do I seem so unreliable?" Becka asked touchily, pulling her hand out of his and making him laugh.

He liked those little, illogical contradictions in her nature and found her funny.

"No, Becka, you don't, but you do look too sweet and too young for a man like me," Bryan answered unapologetically even if amused. He chose to be direct whenever he could.

"I am not so young," she frowned at him. "I've told you I'm already nineteen, haven't I?"

"Yes, you have. I know. But I'm almost thirty-two, almost a lifetime away, and more importantly, I've seen much more of this life than you and not all of it good."

He took her hand back into his and entwined his fingers with hers, making her shiver for a moment.

Both of them felt something like an electric shock run through their intertwined fingers, but neither dared to say anything. They glanced at each other briefly before Becka looked away, trying to mask what she was feeling.

After a few moments, she looked back at him, "I wouldn't have thought you were so old."

She saw his eyebrow rising doubtfully and she hurried to correct herself, "Not that you're old. You aren't. But..."

He started laughing heartily and she stopped her explanations, turning her nose up childishly again.

"You're so funny, and your fuse is so short! It's amazing you get upset so easily. It's refreshing to see someone so natural, not faking every emotion," he said and squeezed her fingers gently.

"You should know it's not a good idea to annoy me," she started in force, but left her statement at that.

"Or what, sweetie?" he asked a bit steely.

She stopped suddenly, glanced behind them, then back at him again with nervous eyes, and whispered, "I can't tell you."

"Now, you've made me curious. Really, really, curious. Are you with the mob or something?" he asked her, only half-joking.

Nothing truly shocked him anymore and he'd learned to take everything in stride, but he liked to know what he was up against and the sooner, the better. He might have had a worthless hide, but it was his, and he had some sort of attachment to it.

"What?" She cried out and stopped in her tracks for a second. Her eyes widened to what seemed the size of small saucers in incredulity at his outrageous idea.

Becka couldn't believe her ears. She wouldn't have ever imagined someone would ask her such a question and she was afraid Bryan was making fun of her.

"Well, you just threatened me..." he started speaking, only to be interrupted.

"I didn't threaten you, you blockhead! I just warned you," she replied with real anger in her voice this time, but he didn't seem to care.

"Same thing," he shrugged nonchalantly.

"No, it isn't," she insisted. "That's not the same thing. And I haven't said anything about the mob. Where did you get such an idea?" she asked in a biting tone.

He glanced at her and saw her face was turning purple.

"But you warned me not to annoy you," he tried to approach it logically and calm her down at the same time, as he felt her temper rising.

"Yes, but that doesn't mean..."

"I understand a threat when I hear one, Becka," he interrupted her forcefully this time. Any kind of playfulness was gone from his voice. "So, what are you going to do to me? Murder me in my sleep?"

"Are you mocking me?" she scowled at his questions and the tone of his voice.

"No, I'm dead serious. I might have a worthless hide, but it's still attached to my back, you know," Bryan replied in a matter-of-fact voice, echoing his earlier thoughts.

"Wait, what do you mean, you have a worthless hide?" she asked confused, completely forgetting the line of conversation for a moment.

"Just something I've been told...," Bryan replied softly, avoiding going into details.

"You know you shouldn't trust people who say things like that," she advised him wisely. "I might not know you, but you don't seem worthless to me. At least, this is one thing I can do well. I'm a good judge of character. I can tell you're much more complicated than you seem and I would guess you have a very speckled past, but you're not worthless at all," she said pensively, more kindly than she had been in their argument just moments ago.

"Wow, you do like to talk." he exclaimed, hearing her delivering a lengthy speech.

Mostly, her words humbled him and he didn't want to let her see it.

"You want me to shut up?" she replied upset. "I can shut up. If it bothers you so much, I can stop talking altogether! It's not a problem for me!"

"No, not at all," he pulled her closer to him and squeezed her fingers tenderly. "I actually like the sound of your voice. It's not one of those voices that sounds like a chime and grates my ears. It's got a low pitch, almost throaty, sexy, I could say. Although, I'm pretty sure that mouth of yours would be good at other things, too, not just talking," he added with measured nonchalance, watching her carefully to see her reaction to such a blunt suggestion.

Shocked, Becka looked up at him for a few moments, her eyes wide again, then she started walking faster, to leave behind what was just said, but forgot about their laced fingers that wouldn't allow her an easy escape. He laughed and matched his stride to hers.

"Come on, don't act like a little virgin. No one is so innocent these days," he tried to smooth her ruffled feathers.

"It's not about being innocent, you ass! It's our first date!" Becka snapped back and rolled her eyes.

"So? You follow the rules? A kiss on the first date, a longer one and first base for the second and sex on the third?"

"I don't follow any rules. I don't know any rules! But if there are any, then you might just forget about getting any kiss today or tomorrow or the day after," Becka replied furiously.

"Why? Am I being punished?" he asked, a quiet chuckle betraying his teasing interest.

She scoffed at the simple suggestion, "Like I'd care to. It's about what I feel and what I want."

"And you feel nothing when it comes to me, is that what you're saying?" he asked her, more curious about her opinion of him so far than at all disappointed with the thought.

It wasn't as if he'd gotten his hopes up for a relationship only to find out he didn't measure up.

"I didn't say that, so, please, don't put words into my mouth!"

"Then what did you say?" he insisted.

"That it might be a possibility. I actually don't appreciate what you said… It was crass and you know it… I think you did it on purpose only I don't know why…"

He waited to see what else she had to say. He found her more fascinating than he ever thought she would be, especially for someone so young.

"You know what, let's have dinner, change the subject and maybe you'll get that kiss," she replied cheerfully trying to appease both of them and save the evening.

"I'm not a child to bribe me with a candy, Becka," he replied evenly, scowling at her.

"Ugh!" she growled. "You're impossible! You choose to misunderstand everything I say."

"Why, because I don't let you treat me in the way you would treat the children you normally date?" Bryan retorted.

Becka stopped and turned to him, in disbelief yet again, "You know what, Bryan? I think you've got a complex, and it's a big one. You have a big chip on your shoulder, don't you? I don't understand though. If you're so stressed out by our age gap, why did you ask me out? You should have played it safe and spared yourself the trouble of putting up with a *'child'*!" she ended her tirade almost shouting.

A slight breeze ruffled the leaves in the trees.

Bryan didn't say anything for a few moments but thought to himself, *well, damn. She's got a point there!* However, he decided not to let her see she touched a nerve or she'd guessed what he thought and kept staring her down, which didn't have the desired effect. She didn't back down.

"I don't have a complex," he replied stubbornly in the end. "But I don't like to be patted on the head like some five-year-old either. I don't like to be told if I'm good I'll get a cookie."

"Oh, really? And you think I'm going to believe you?"

The man let her comment hang in the air for a few moments, unsure what to believe of her behavior. It was like she'd tried to provoke him and it didn't seem plausible.

"You're a little hellion, Becka. I'm almost twice your size…"

"What's that got to do with anything? Unless you intend to fight me?" she asked as if she wanted to know how that would end, half challenging him, half warning him off.

Bryan laughed heartily, brought her hand to his lips and kissed her fingers.

"Of course, not. Don't be silly. You just astonish me. Usually, women are more careful around me," he replied amused.

"How come?" Becka asked.

"Well, if you want to know, they avoid me. Most of them. But no woman has ever threatened me or provoked me like you do…" he said, watching her as if she had been an odd exhibit in a museum.

"Oh, for God's sake!" Becka snapped, throwing her hands into the air dramatically. "I haven't threatened you! Can't you get it through your thick skull?"

He opened his mouth to say something, but she reached up and covered his mouth with her palm, shaking her head at the same time to stop him from adding anything else to what he'd already said. He obeyed mutely and just watched her.

"Could we leave it at that, Bryan? Believe me it was not a threat, okay. Maybe, one day, I'll tell you what's all that about but not today, okay?"

"Okay, not a threat," he said after she took her hand off his mouth.

***

The hostess showed them to a table close to the lake, where Bryan courteously pulled her chair and helped her to sit at the table. After she was seated, Becka looked at the lake wistfully.

A dozen boats had set sail out on the lake that day and the shiny surface of the water was peppered with white sails, canoes and all sorts of other boats.

Becka was crazy about sailing and yet she'd rarely had the chance to go out on the lake lately. Matt was the only one with his own boat and he hadn't had enough time to take her out sailing that summer because he'd been so busy with his work all the time.

Bryan sat down at his turn and gazed at her. It wasn't difficult to spot the wistfulness in her eyes and he understood what she wanted.

The man took her narrow hand in his broader one and stroking the back of her hand tenderly in a comforting gesture to distract her from her yearning, he said softly, "If you want we can go sailing on the lake tomorrow morning or in the afternoon. I understand the weather will keep so we'll have another nice day. Not a spot of clouds. I have access to a little pocket cruiser you might like."

"Really?" Becka's entire face lit up with excitement. That meant the summer might not go to waste after all.

Bryan was fascinated again. Yes, he'd liked her beautifully arched lips enough to ask her out on a date, but now, he saw much more than that.

Becka was a beautiful woman indeed. She didn't have any use for artifices, and that puzzled him. Most women would wear a lot of makeup to be attractive, especially when they were very young and wanted to appear sophisticated.

Becka's makeup was subtle to the point of nonexistence. She might have used something on her eyelashes, but he couldn't be sure. He could be sure, though, that she didn't wear any lipstick and not even a trace of perfume. And yet, she smelled like wild flowers. Leaning in closer to her, he realised it was her hair that smelled of flowers.

"Hmmm…"

"What?" she asked startled.

"Nothing, nothing," he waved her worries away. "I was just wondering what shampoo you used because I've never smelled anything like that," Bryan explained to her.

"Really? My shampoo? We were talking about sailing," she chided him for such a silly side-note and he could tell she was disappointed.

"Yes, we were," he reassured her. "My offer still stands, even if you don't want to go tomorrow. My question about your shampoo was just curiosity. That scent is amazing," he specified.

"All right, then, let's satisfy your curiosity. It's a shampoo made especially for me by one of my cousins, that's why it's so unique. She chose some flowers that go well with my skin and hair. But that's not important now, Bryan. Yes, I want to go on the boat with you tomorrow. I'll skip my classes, not a problem."

"Just like that?" he wondered.

He wasn't ready to accept it had been so easy to get her to go out with him again. It wasn't usually that way with other women. He had to work a little more.

"Yep, just like that," she replied smiling at him. "I'm truly crazy about sailing, you see, and I haven't had any chance to go on the water this year. That's why I actually took classes this summer because I knew I'd die of boredom otherwise. At least, having to go to school takes my mind of what I've missed," the young woman explained to him.

"Who takes you sailing usually?" Bryan asked, feeling the sting of jealousy rising in his throat. He'd known he must have had some competition but he'd preferred to push the thought aside.

"Matt, but he seems to be busier than ever this summer and every time I tried to ask to go sailing, he never had the time," she said with regret in her voice.

"Who's Matt?" Bryan asked now truly envious of the unknown man. "You said you didn't have any boyfriends, sweetie," he pointed out.

"Oh, no, Matt's not a boyfriend. He's just one of my cousins," she answered to him hastily, but she didn't add anything more when the waitress interrupted them to take their order.

Bryan waited patiently until the waitress left with their orders and asked, pretending to be absent-minded, "You have lots of cousins?"

"You might say that," Becka replied turning to him. She'd been watching the lake again. "I have five cousins and two siblings. You?"

Bryan shrugged and replied, "I might have a cousin somewhere in the west of the country, but I haven't seen him in ten years at least. No siblings."

"Oh, that's bad. Aren't you lonely?" Becka asked, feeling sorry for him.

She couldn't imagine how it would be like not having someone to plot or quarrel with. She'd always counted on having someone to turn to if she needed company or help.

"Not really," he mumbled and leaned back to let the waitress who had returned with their drinks to put the glasses on the table.

The beer was cold and felt good after the hot afternoon they'd had. After a few moments of idle silence, while she watched the boats on the lake and he gazed at her, he continued, "We can leave in the morning if you want, and return in the evening, take a picnic with us…"

"I'd love to!" she jumped at the idea and continued speaking quickly in an excitement she couldn't even begin to contain. "Let's do it! How early do you want to leave? I hope it won't be at the crack of dawn. I can't function so early in the morning," Becka said playfully.

She was serious though. She avoided waking up early every time she could.

"No worries, not so early," he replied with a smile in his voice. "We can wait till eight-thirty or nine… What do you say if I come and get you at eight-thirty? … Or are you afraid to tell me where you live?" Bryan asked when he saw her reflect upon his words.

"Ah, no, no, it's not that," Becka waved his concern away as not important. "I don't mind if you know where I live. You don't give off that serial killer vibe …," she said, making his eyebrows instantly go up at her strange ideas. "I was just thinking whether eight-thirty would be too early or not, but I think I can survive getting up at seven."

For a moment, Bryan just stared at her. He wasn't even able to think of a reply as he was still stumped about the serial killer reference.

The man didn't even know or could have imagined that there was such a thing like a vibe specific to a serial killer. After a few moments of shock, he shook his head trying to clear his mind and only then registered what else she said.

"You really like your sleep," he laughed.

"You don't even know the half of it," Becka merrily replied. "I'm a bit of a night owl, you see. I like to go to bed late at night so it's no wonder I can't get up early in the morning," she shrugged.

"How do you manage with school?" Bryan asked taking another sip of his drink.

"Oh, that's another story altogether," she waved her hand dismissively and sipped from her beer as well. "Actually, it's not that much of a mystery," she suddenly decided to answer. "I simply choose my courses with two things in mind: they can't be too early in the morning and, of course, they have to be interesting… You know," she said with a conspiring air, "I can't even declare a major because I don't really know what to focus on. I like too many things, you see, and…"

"So you're undecided about your future," he concluded, stroking her long fingers with carefully manicured, short nails.

Bryan didn't think that her indecision was too much of a problem at her age. She still had the time to decide what direction to follow in her life.

"Actually, I do know what I want to do in the future," she corrected him. "Not that it would do me any good…." Becka mumbled grudgingly.

His strokes were playing havoc on her sensitive nerves and confused her thoughts, stealing away her senses toward a drowsy concentration on the soft, pleasant caresses. It wasn't as if she'd never met a guy who tried to play doctor with her, but this one was different.

Bryan was totally unlike the guys who asked her out before. She'd been completely indifferent to her dates in the past and she'd even convinced herself it was her fault she couldn't feel anything because probably she was a cold person. What happened now contradicted her beliefs. Her body reacted very strongly to this man and without the usual annoyance she felt whenever someone wanted to touch her.

"Why not?" he asked, mesmerized by the chain of emotions passing over her expressive face.

He was certain she had to be the worst poker player in the world. Almost everything she thought was clearly visible on her face for all to see.

She looked at him startled, as if she hadn't expected him to talk. Then, she realized that she had said too much in her pleasure-induced near-trance.

"It might not be possible to do what I want," she said after a while. "There are some conditions... and even people that are much better than I didn't succeed... so...."

"Don't sell yourself short," he cut her hesitation short. "You might succeed even if others have failed. You want to elaborate though so that I understand and probably help..."

"Oh, no, I can't," she interrupted him. "It's not something I'm supposed to say, you see?"

"Why not?" he frowned. He never liked foggy matters and, apparently, the young woman was involved in a lot of such things.

"Because I can't," she pleaded for his understanding.

"Are you mixed up in something?" he scowled at her, not because he didn't want to get involved with a woman involved in nefarious affairs, but because of a sudden urge to get her out of trouble. Bryan wasn't the helpful type of man but she'd wormed her way into his heart. That troubled him.

"Oh, no, not that, of course, don't be silly," she laughed with easy cheerfulness, dispelling his dark thoughts. "It's just a family thing... Can we talk about something else?" she waved the subject away.

"People date so they can get to know each other, Becka. If you keep secrets...." Bryan tried a different way to get to the heart of the matter.

"Oh, come on, like you've told me your secrets!" she cried out frustrated. "I won't fall so easily for that sort of thing."

"You haven't asked me anything," Bryan answered with a smile tugging at the corner of his mouth. "But I have asked, you see, so, of course, I expect answers," he nodded to put more weight on his words.

Becka traced the contour of the glass with a finger pensively. She was trying to figure out some way to turn his expectations against himself.

"But why do you get to ask first and not me?" she glanced at him with suddenly sharp eyes.

"All right, ladies first," he generously gave in, as if he'd been doing her a favor. "You ask your questions first and then I'll want my answers," Bryan said with a finality in his tone that promised he would offer her no escape from holding up her end of the deal.

Becka took a few moments to think about it, but finally admitted with disappointment, "I don't know what to ask or... how to ask," she said, glancing back at him.

"Then I don't know what answers you want," Bryan mused at her unwilling to say anything without being specifically asked.

She frowned for a second, then smiled as if she had just discovered the secret of life, "All right, tell me everything about you."

"Huh, you don't ask for much, do you?" he laughed at her ingenuity.

"I think my question covers everything, so start talking," Becka gesticulated. "I'm afraid you might not even finish today and you'll have to continue tomorrow and the day after tomorrow...," Becka laughed, happy that she found the perfect solution to elude his questions.

"You're something else," he said through laughter and took her hand again.

He looked at her fingers, stroking each of them slowly until he realized she was shivering.

"Did I make you uncomfortable?" he asked, glancing at her eyes.

"No… no, you don't. I'm just not… used to… that…" she tried to explain.

"Hmm, you make me wonder how many boyfriends you've had and how clumsy they were," he mused under his breath, but she still heard him.

She took a few seconds to think, tilting her head to the side in a gesture he'd noticed about her earlier and found endearing, before she said, "I think there were four and yes, they were clumsy and went directly for the kill."

"And what did you say?" he asked, holding her gaze with interest, imagining his little hellion crush the laughable attempts of horny teenagers.

"Of course, I said no," she answered haughtily.

"But not always," he surmised. He was a realist after all.

"Why not?" she shrugged. "Believe me, it wasn't worth the trouble," she replied and frowned, at the same time.

Becka didn't understand where he was going with his line of questions. She wasn't very comfortable with them.

His sharp gaze held hers before he let go of her hand. Leaning back on his chair, Bryan analysed her for a few moments. His disbelief was palpable.

Then he asked her in a voice full of awe, "You want to tell me you've never been with a man… or a boy before?"

"It's not that I want to say so, but it seems I've already had. Is that a problem for you, Bryan?

You prefer experienced women and you don't date little bookworms like me?" Becka asked him snappily. She hated labels especially when they were attached to her.

"Where did that come from?" he asked, puzzled by her sudden outburst.

"You said…"

"Wait a minute, sweetie! I haven't said anything about you being a bookworm," Bryan interrupted her by putting his hand up sharply to stop her from talking over him.

She waved his concern aside and replied, "It's not a big deal. There were others who said so, so I'm not surprised that you might think the same way too," she shrugged his excuses off.

"Don't lump me in with the others, Becka, all right?" he leaned towards her, stressing his words so she could get his message loud and clear. "I'm not a stupid teenager who's looking to score with a different girl every night and add notches to my belt. And besides, you don't strike me as a bookworm," he clarified, always fixing her with his determined eyes. "Not even a little."

"Well, truth be told, I am sort of a bookworm," she admitted sheepishly, her gaze trailing to the side to avoid his own.

Despite it being the truth, it was a particularly sensitive button for her.

"I prefer reading to spending time with my classmates. Some of them can't share a thought between them and…" Becka shrugged again. "Look, I tried, okay… but it was so damn boring to be around them all the time," she protested with large gestures.

Bryan burst into laughter and said, "Let's hope I'm not as boring as them and you won't get sick of me too soon."

"You know I've never said anything like that," Becka said reproachfully, a little concerned about them being at odds all the time.

She'd never been so snappy and contradictory with anyone before. She didn't understand what made her react so strangely when it came to Bryan.

"No, you haven't, I admit it," Bryan agreed with a nod of his head. "Anyway, I'm sure I can show you some things neither of those kids could," Bryan replied with a wolfish smile that made a shiver trickle down her spine.

His words, as well as his meaningful smile, took her aback for a few seconds.

Bryan was as blond as a Viking or rather, the way she'd always imagined Vikings. His icy blue eyes seemed to shoot arrows her way now and then, and she felt each one of them somewhere in her belly. It was like a constant attack on her senses.

Whenever he would touch her hand, and stroke her skin with those long, thick, and calloused fingers, little sparks ignited in all her nervous endings. It made her feel strange. She found herself wanting something more from him and at the same time, she was afraid of what she might get in the end.

Becka was aware Bryan wasn't the kind of man with whom she could play games and hope he would stop if she said no in the end. He didn't seem like the kind of man who would take any sort of games kindly. This man was too intense and too seasoned for that. One thing was very clear to her, there were risks involved in such a relationship and yet, she didn't want to back out of it.

Becka also had the unsettling feeling Bryan was aware of what he was doing to her and he enjoyed the results immensely. Since she wasn't sure yet if he was serious or just having a little fun with her, she hated herself for being so transparent and offering everything to him on a silver platter.

What bothered her more was the fact that she was painfully aware of what was going on. That didn't mean she could do a thing to change the way she reacted.

Becka was simply stunned that she could experience such intense sensations just because he was stroking her fingers. It wasn't like she had never dated and she hadn't had any kind of experience on the scene. However, she was positive none of the guys she had gone out with in the past could make her feel a tenth of what she was feeling now, and that without too much effort on Bryan's part.

The young woman took her glass and sipped slowly from the cold beer, just to give herself time to come up with something to say. She thought hard and well but she couldn't find anything worth mentioning.

At the same time, she was staring at the tablecloth as if she could find some inspiration there. However, her mind was blank, which only made her more furious with herself. She was acting like a fool.

She couldn't bear the thought that a man could make her forget everything in a matter of seconds. That woman there wasn't anything like her. Where was her witty spirit and her deflective skills?

Bryan touched her hand gently again and made her snap out of her thoughts and look up at him. He was smiling at her.

"Don't try too hard," he advised her in a soft voice. "It's not rocket science, it's just a date. We can talk about anything and everything. It's up to you. No one can make you say or do something you don't want, all right, Becka? Let's find a neutral subject. For instance, why don't you tell me about those classes you're taking," Bryan suggested.

Becka pulled her hand away and let it fall into her lap to cut off the flux of emotion. Then, she cleared her throat before saying, "I'm taking some art classes this summer. They're just optional courses, you know. I just needed something to do," she said shrugging her shoulders and Bryan noted that the gesture seemed to be defining for her.

Becka continued, unaware of his thoughts, "Everybody in the family is busy with something right now and I was feeling a little… left aside, if you know what I mean."

Bryan, who knew very well how it felt to be left aside, nodded and, glancing at her left, said, "It looks like our food is here."

They both kept silent while the waitress laid the food on the table, and then they said their polite *'thank you'* and attacked their plates.

Happy she finally had something to do, Becka started cutting into her juicy steak with enthusiasm. It looked exactly as she wanted it. She hoped it would also taste as good as it seemed.

She hadn't had too much to eat that day. She'd lost the muffin and the toasted bagel when she went to buy the shirt for Bryan. With the flood in the kitchen at home, she hadn't had time to prepare anything to eat that afternoon. Now, she was famished and didn't need to fake her enthusiasm.

"It was refreshing to hear you wanted a steak and not a salad with the dressing on the side," Bryan told her after he swallowed his first bite. "I hate seeing women go hungry just because fashion says they have to be skinny with no curves. I, for one, can't understand why anyone would want a woman with no curves."

"Huh… you won't see me doing that," Becka replied, glancing at him and at the same time, cutting another piece of the steak. "Skipping meals, I mean, or eating only salad," she specified. "Of course, I enjoy a salad as much as the next person, don't get me wrong. But, especially, if I didn't have time to eat all day, like today, I do enjoy a good meal. It's not like I'd ever be skinny anyhow and I don't think it's worth crying about something you can't have," she said and this time she shrugged only one shoulder.

His eyes lingered on her for a few moments. Then he said very matter of fact, "I don't think you have anything to complain about. You're just the perfect size."

"Thank you, you are so kind," she retorted sarcastically.

Becka was sure he was either trying to be polite or was making fun of her in a covert way.

"No, really, you are. Believe me, I can't wait to trace the shape of your body with my hands."

At his words, she simply dropped the fork onto the plate, not even registering the clank, which resonated far enough to make people turn their heads towards their table. Her mouth formed a perfect 'o', which prompted him to laugh heartily.

"Come on, don't tell me you didn't expect me to go in that direction," he said on a playful tone, trying to make her feel at ease. He failed.

Becka tried to say something, swallowed hard, and tried again. Nothing came out. She was speechless.

"Are you all right?" he asked her, concerned by now.

If the situation amused him for the a few seconds, now it worried him and seriously.

Bryan was afraid he'd pushed too soon because she seemed completely overwhelmed. He would hate himself if he had pushed her away with his impatience. She was the first woman he had been attracted to in months and he didn't feel like losing her before having a chance to start something.

Becka nodded hesitantly and then, standing up abruptly, she said, "Will you excuse me for a moment?"

He stood too, setting his fork and knife down on the plate. Now the man was worried and his worry showed in the frown between his eyebrows.

"You're coming back, aren't you?" he couldn't help but ask her.

"Yes, of course, I will. Where do you think I'm going? I'm just going to the ladies' room not fleeing the scene," she glanced at him and nodded.

Then, Becka hurried in the direction of the ladies' room without looking behind. Inside the ladies' room, after checking to see if she was alone, she leaned heavily on the first sink, which didn't seem wet, and looked carefully at herself in the mirror.

Her face was flushed and there was a new shine in her eyes, which worried her a little. Becka closed her eyes for a moment, breathed deeply and thought, *"All right, this is the one, I think. Maybe not tonight, but soon, definitely. The very first one who made me feel like doing it. It makes sense..."*

With the decision finally made, Becka splashed some water on her face, then straightened up and dried her face and hands carefully.

She weighed her decision for a few seconds more before leaving the washroom to go back to the table, where Bryan was waiting for her, sipping slowly from his beer.

His eyes found her at once, and he watched her until she got to the table. When she was close enough, he stood up respectfully to help her sit down.

That was something she hadn't seen anywhere else but in movies until then, and she felt flattered he would go through all that trouble. Becka also admired the fluidity of his movements, which showed he was a man who would go through rigorous training, maybe every day.

She sat down with an encouraging smile and took her own glass of beer to wet her lips in the bitter liquid. Her smile still showed over the rim of her glass, a little more boldly now, and the look in her eyes made him feel that pull towards her stronger.

His cock stirred in his pants and drew his attention to the sudden uncomfortable tightness. Bryan became aware of two things. First of all, he was happy he was sitting down and the tablecloth hid his awkward state. He wouldn't have liked for her to notice how far she pushed him, especially because of how she had reacted earlier to his suggestion of a less than innocent nature. The second thing was he would definitely have her, sooner or later, Bryan promised to himself. That wasn't a woman he could just let pass by and out of his life too soon.

He needed her at a visceral level and not only in his bed. He needed to spend enough time with her to see exactly what that pull between them meant and he was determined to steal that time if it was necessary.

"Are you up for a stroll along the lake after the meal?" he asked her, nodding towards the promenade busy with people. "It's not too windy and it's still warm out for this hour of the evening."

Becka nodded and added in a playful tone, "I hope you'll buy me some dessert as well, though."

Bryan laughed heartily and shook his head as if he couldn't believe her.

"I have to say you're the first woman in years who's asked me for dessert. I wasn't even sure women ate cakes or ice-cream anymore."

"This one does," Becka told him, leaning towards him as if she was confessing a sin. "If possible at the same time, the better. You know, a hot chocolate cake with a scoop or two of ice-cream on top… However, for future reference, it's not a good idea to mention your previous relationships to a woman," she winked at him as if she'd parted with a secret. "We have this thing, you know," Becka waved her hand. "Maybe it's a quirk, but we prefer to think we're the only one that ever existed in a man's life."

"Dully noted," Bryan replied with amusement and grinned. "I'll refrain from making comparisons from now on, although I'd have thought you'd be flattered by the comparison."

She shook her head at him and with a large wave of her hand, she replied, "Not really. You're far, far from the truth. You see, I might conclude you think I'm a glutton, and that won't do. No, it won't do at all."

"Oh, no, baby, I wouldn't think something like that. I've always wanted to see a woman with a healthy appetite and here you are. It seems I've finally found one. You might be totally unique," Bryan retorted as he enjoyed some more of his beer without taking his eyes off her.

"Of course, I'm unique. Everyone's unique, Bryan. There aren't two people alike," Becka said a little too loud and a head or two turned to them. Neither Becka nor Bryan noticed.

"If only you knew...," he said wistfully shaking his head. "Too many people try to emulate someone else and in the end, you just end up with so many copies of the same person that you're sick of them," he continued and something like regret registered in his voice.

"Wow, Bryan, I don't even want to know what kind of women you've dated if you have such a good opinion about my sex," Becka replied with awe in her voice. "Luckily for you, I'm here now. And as you mentioned, I'm one of a kind," she joked.

"Yeah, you are, Becka, and I mean to keep you," he answered back, suddenly with a serious tone.

His words sent a shiver down her spine. His seriousness showed he wasn't a man she should trifle with.

"Should I be worried?" Becka tried to joke, but he could see in her eyes a little glimmer of concern because of the intensity of his statement.

"I'm not a stalker, Becka, don't worry about that. I meant only to say I want everything between us to go just fine so I can have more time with you, that's all," Bryan explained patiently to ease her concern.

"Ah, all right then. We'll see then, won't we?" she stated very matter-of-factly.

Bryan nodded and seeing she'd already finished her steak, he waved for the waitress.

"So, what would you like for dessert?" he asked her, as he handed her the dessert menu, which had been left on the table.

Becka opened the menu and perused the dessert choices at length until she found something to suit her desires best.

"I think the triple chocolate brownie with ice-cream. Told you, already. I love chocolate cake and ice-cream. My favorite. You?"

"Decadent, I like it. I'll take the same. Something more to drink?"

Becka looked at the lake, then at the approaching waitress, and only then, found the courage to meet his eyes and say, "I don't really drink, Bryan. Even this beer was too much, I think."

"Damn it, you're only nineteen. You're barely legal to drink. I'm sorry, Becka, it's slipped my mind. Maybe you want a soft drink?" he asked, troubled that he hadn't noticed something so important.

He kicked himself mentally for letting himself so engrossed with her that he would make such a mistake. Usually, he would let nothing slip past him.

Bryan knew he couldn't afford to make mistakes if he wanted that relationship to last. It wasn't as if she hadn't had her choice of men. He was just one in a sea of tens, probably.

"Yes, I'd like a soft drink or maybe just sparkling water. I think sparkling water is perfect."

"Sure?"

When she nodded, he gave their order to the waitress. After the waitress left, he took her hand and kissed her fingers. He seemed obsessed with her fingers and she didn't know what to believe.

"I'll keep in mind not to have alcoholic beverages around you, all right?"

She laughed merrily and eased his worries.

"Come on, Bryan. You can drink, it's not like the law forbids you to drink around me," she laughed. "I like a glass of champagne now and then. That I like when there's something to celebrate. I'm not too fond of anything else. The taste is not for me."

"So, I'll buy you only champagne, Becka. The best kind, of course. I'm sure I'll be able to afford it if you drink only on special occasions," he said laughing.

They spoke of everything and nothing in particular for the remainder of the dinner and after he paid, he took her hand and led her to the shore of the lake for a romantic evening stroll.

The sun was setting, but the promenade was still bustling with people, which Bryan resented deeply. He wanted to have her only to himself and the people milling around intruded on his time with her.

Becka felt the shift in his mood and wondered what could have possibly brought on such a change from the light-hearted, content mood from just mere minutes ago. He was almost brooding.

"Is something wrong, Bryan?"

"Too many people, that's all, Becka. I'd have liked to be alone with you," he admitted openly.

Becka just seemed to have a strange effect on him, making him reveal things he wouldn't normally tell women, especially on a first date. His preservation spirit was strong enough to stop him doing such mistakes.

"Well, this place is full almost all the time, you know," Becka dismissed the people around with a large wave of her hand. "It's a favorite place for strolls, especially in the evening," she said, trying to appease him.

"I know, of course. That doesn't mean I have to like it, do I?" he replied tersely, even though he was aware it wasn't her fault the place was so popular.

"Well, if we go sailing tomorrow, we'll be alone for some time," she pointed out, in another attempt to cheer him up.

"We are definitely going," Bryan said. "I hope you haven't changed your mind," he turned to her to see the answer in her eyes.

She shook her head and squeezed his fingers reassuringly, a gesture he enjoyed. In the spur of the moment, he leaned towards her and kissed her lips softly.

That first kiss didn't last more than a few seconds, but the pleasant, electric tingle he felt when he touched her lips was stronger than he'd expected.

Both of them stopped, still close enough to feel the warmth of each other's lips and Becka stared at him with eyes full of wonder. It was barely a kiss, but she felt it as if it had been much more than that. The tingling she had felt earlier seemed like a pale reminder now.

When he pulled her to him tightly, she went along. She didn't even think of resisting. She was impatient to taste more of those low vibrations which made her body hum. She found herself completely stretched along his body, every hard plane of his chest and abdomen burning through her dress.

Bryan kept her very close as if he'd wanted to leave his mark on her and she didn't mind. His lips touched hers, traced the shape of her mouth unhurriedly. His mouth was trying to learn the texture of every cell in the sensitive skin he was tasting. His hot tongue touched the delicate surface of her lips, stroking them slowly, as if they'd had all the time in the world to indulge in each other.

The world outside ceased to exist for both of them. Deeply immersed in their own world, nothing else mattered but only what they could get from each other.

The people strolling around them became invisible and any kind of noise drowned in the background as they listened to the rhythm of their hearts and to the blood pulsing in their ears.

Their lips touched harder and sought a way to become one. Their tongues dueled and caressed one another, at times slowly, unhurriedly, tasting one another, exploring one another and creating sensations. At times, they duelled violently, as if they'd feared they had no time left and every second mattered.

Bryan bit sharply on her bottom lip, making her exhale with a whimper, then sucked her abused lip into his mouth to lavish and nurse it with strokes of his tongue, swallowing the moan escaping from her throat and making it part of himself. His voracious fingers played with the skin covered by the flimsy cloth of her dress and pressed harder whenever he expected more from her.

Her fingers dug into the hard muscles of his shoulders, trying to find support and keep her balance. Becka was caught in the middle of a violent storm and was teetering on the edge of the unknown. Her mind was caught in a whirl of sensations and that made her unable to think about anything else but the greedy demanding mouth, teaching hers ruthlessly what a true kiss meant.

The young woman had the feeling she'd finally left her teen years behind and she was on the brink of maturity. She was in the arms of a man able to show her what she'd longed for, over the last few years when she felt so restless.

That wasn't just about the conditions her great-grandma had put on the trust fund. It was much more than that.

When they finally came up for air, Becka was panting heavily and she was trembling. Even Bryan had to gulp a mouthful of air. Then, he smiled wolfishly at her, with that smile, which seemed to belong exclusively to him, then tilted his head and bit the spot between her neck and collarbone, stroking it quickly with his tongue when he heard her sharp intake of breath at the sudden pain. He suckled on the skin, making her forget about the sting she'd just felt, thrusting her from a world of pain and fear to one of bewitched pleasure.

Becka was throbbing everywhere. She knew now that she wanted his touch all over her body. She needed that ruthless mouth of his on her, on her most sensitive spots.

Becka opened her mouth to say something along those lines, but Bryan put a finger over her lips and stopped her.

"Becka, we have an audience," he said and pointed to the left.

He glanced at the left as well and when she turned her eyes in that direction, she noticed several teenage girls clustered together, watching them with curiosity and laughing like they'd never seen a woman and a man kissing before.

Becka couldn't hear what they were saying but she imagined it wasn't something she'd have liked to hear. At a loss for words, she looked up at Bryan, waiting for his opinion.

"I think we should move on," he said softly and after stroking her cheek with his rough, calloused knuckles, he took her hand in his and slowly started towards the other end of the promenade, where the lake was shimmering in the sunset light.

CHAPTER THREE

Bryan arrived at Becka's house five minutes earlier than the time they'd agreed upon. He decided to wait until eight thirty before ringing her bell.

He remembered very well how particular she'd been about the time of their date and how much she loved her sleep. He assumed she would also need time to get ready and he was determined to give it to her.

Bryan didn't want to start his day with Becka on a sore note. Spending his entire day with Becka, as well as developing a relationship with her, seemed very promising and he wanted to cling to his chance.

On top of that, he had his own expectations for their second date. He knew he was probably hoping for far too much and his expectations were maybe too high, but he still wanted to fulfill them or at least a part of them.

At eight-thirty precisely, he rang the bell at the door. The sound of her doorbell stirred the butterflies in his stomach to life and they churned with anticipation and anxiety. At the same time, a grin flourished on his lips as the theme from *Jaws* beamed in his ears.

Bryan wouldn't have expected to hear that song playing on her doorbell. Had it been something else, like *We Wish You a Merry*

Christmas or the theme of *Love Actually*, for instance, he'd have understood. Every time he discovered that there was more to Becka than met the eye and that was what made him so adamant not to lose her.

Bryan could hear the echo of the thrilling theme fill the house. That sound made him more anxious to see Becka open the door and beam widely at him with that bright smile of hers, which always reached her chocolate eyes.

Unfortunately, that didn't happen. The man strained his ears and listened attentively, eager to hear the sound of her hurried steps coming to the door or even the noise of a shoe thrown into the wall or anything at all. To his disappointment, no sound came from inside the house and his hopes plummeted hard.

When it flashed through his mind the thought that she might have just made a fool out of him and had no intention of seeing him again, Bryan frowned and gritted his teeth.

He was convinced he'd walked her to her own door the previous night. He'd even watched her go inside. He hadn't seen her use a key to open the door, but she'd waved at him and closed the door behind herself.

It wasn't like he'd left her standing on the steps of a house of her choice so she could walk to another door after he'd left.

The thought he'd been duped was unbearable. He'd been there before and didn't have any desire to revisit the experience. This time, though, the hurt ran deeper because he had truly thought they had had a great time together and it worried him that that impression might have been one sided.

Bryan didn't want to travel down that path, but he had to admit that, although she'd gone inside that house the night before with that air of an owner, it didn't mean she couldn't have just visited the house of one of her friends, who would have left earlier that morning, before he arrived, or who just kept quiet like a mouse, waiting for him to give up and leave.

His anger increased more at the thought of having been played like that. Bryan choked under the pressure of his fury. He wasn't mad only at her because she'd made a fool out of him. He was furious with himself, as well, for falling for her act.

Furious, he punched the door frame with such force that the hardwood scraped his knuckles and he started bleeding.

He swore and cursed himself viciously. Damn it, he wasn't a green, young man and he should have known better. Much better.

Becka had seemed too nice and too beautiful for the likes of him and he shouldn't have pinned any kind of hopes on her because he didn't have that right.

After all, he'd been told that enough throughout his life and he thought he'd learned that lesson. Yet, it seemed that he was only lying to himself.

The man glanced at his watch again and noticed that almost five minutes had passed since he rang the bell the first time. Still there wasn't any sound coming from inside the house.

That was the last drop. It convinced him he'd been wrong and his worst fears had turned out to be true. He'd just been played.

Bryan turned his head and glanced at the car he'd parked in the driveway that morning. He hesitated for a few moments, but then thought he'd better leave since there wasn't anything else for him to do there. If she didn't want to see him, then he couldn't do anything to force her.

In that instant, something hardened inside him and shaking his head, he stubbornly decided to try his chance again. He rang the bell once more.

He listened again to the musical sound bouncing off the inner walls of the house, but he still couldn't hear any kind of movement from inside.

That was the final straw. Bryan had to admit defeat. He leaned in and pressed his head on the front door in a moment of weakness. His shoulders stooped.

A slip of a girl had tricked him and he had to live with that. Well, it wasn't the first time and it probably wouldn't be the last. Weak consolation!

Furious, he gritted his teeth, clenched and unclenched his fists and then, finally, he turned around and made a beeline to his car. His stride was determined and his anger showed in every heavy step he took.

He was just opening his car door when he heard her shout breathlessly, "Bryan, wait! ... Just give me the time to get there... Don't leave now!"

The man sharply turned to the sound of her voice and astonishment glimmered in his hard eyes. His puzzlement increased more when he spotted Becka running down the street towards him on wobbly legs.

Her face was almost blue because of her effort and he could see she was close to exhaustion. That didn't stop her and she still tried to smile at him.

Becka held her hand on the right side of her body where a stitch had been bothering her for the last ten minutes. She hadn't thought she'd be there in time, even though she ran as fast as she could.

He waved at her to slow down and stop running. A bright, wide smile spread on her lips. She was grateful that she could finally stop. That was the smile he'd been waiting impatiently for that entire morning.

She stopped abruptly and bent, her hands pressing desperately on her knees. Then she started panting, gulping noisily for air. It was clear she wasn't trained for jogging.

Becka was only about three houses far away from hers, but Bryan hurried to her and reached her in no time. Worried, he slipped his arm around her waist to support her and brushed the heavy hair away from her face.

"What have you been trying to do?" Bryan asked Becka, seeing the traces her sustained effort had left on her face and feeling her tremble in his arms. "Are you training for the marathon or what? Don't you know you should take it gradually?"

"I… had… to… do… something…," she replied with difficulty, wheezing the words as she tried to draw her breath.

Bryan allowed her to recover and didn't press further. He was content just to have her there with him. For the moment, it was enough. It was much more than what he'd had a few moments before when he thought he'd been deceived.

"When I saw I was going to be late for our date… I had to run to make it here in time," Becka finally said when she could breathe easier.

There was still a strain in her voice and Bryan stopped her, touching her lips gently with his fingers.

"Okay, baby," Bryan told her, "just breathe now and you'll tell me everything later."

Becka nodded and started to walk towards her door, but her legs chose that very moment to start shaking violently and she almost fell on her face. Luckily, Bryan was still there and had one arm around her, ready to save her from taking a dive on the hard pavement.

He shook his head, then picked her forcefully up into his arms and without a word, he carried back to her house. His long strides were eating the distance with ease. With a faint yelp of surprise, Becka slipped her arms around his neck.

"How long did you run?" he asked when they made it in front of her house and he stopped to look at her.

Becka had her head comfortably nesting on his shoulder and her nose was close to his neck. She was just enjoying the smell of his skin when she heard him speak. His voice startled her and she felt a faint trace of guilt, but pushed it aside without too much concern. It took her a moment to process his words once she broke from her reverie.

"Well, about ten blocks, I think, or maybe more...," she answered uncertainly. She couldn't remember exactly.

Bryan looked down at her with astonishment.

"Why the hell would you run such a long distance? Especially if you don't have the training? What went through your mind?"

"How do you know I don't have the training?" Becka pouted, choosing to deflect only a part of his questions.

"Well, the shaking legs and the cramp you have on your right side were clear indications, Becka. I don't need to be an expert to see you don't normally run for so long," he replied laughing, although his concern was far from appeased. "If you run at all," he specified and his right eyebrow shot up inquiringly.

"Ah! Right...," her voice trailed off, as she lost herself in thought.

"Still with me, baby?"

She looked up at him and smiled.

"Yes, still here, of course. I was just thinking."

"Yeah, I noticed that," Bryan replied amused gazing into her eyes. "What were you thinking about?"

"All right, then," Becka said. "I was wondering whether I should come clean or not."

At that, Bryan's left eyebrow rose. He didn't expect a confession from her. He didn't expect her to have something to confess.

"I don't have any training and I actually hate jogging," Becka continued, making him burst into laughter.

He had expected to hear something else and the innocence of her confession was music to his ears.

"No, you see, I had to leave this morning and since I didn't get your phone number to let you know I wouldn't be here when you came, I had to hurry back," she explained after she slapped his shoulder for laughing at her.

"That's very considerate of you," Bryan answered quietly after a second, uncertain of what he should say.

It was the first time in his life that someone had thought to show him any kind of consideration. People either feared him and avoided him from afar or didn't give a damn about him. Either way, no one had ever taken his feelings into consideration before that day and he felt humbled.

The cynic in him was a bit stumped and didn't know how to react. He was deep in uncharted territory there and he felt as if he'd had to act out a part in a play, but he didn't know his lines.

"If you want, you can put me down so I can open the door," he heard Becka's voice and turned his eyes to her, taking in her dishevelled appearance, bright eyes and her cheeks still violently red.

"If you give me the key, I'll open the door without putting you down," he said with a hint of playfulness and a smile to match.

"Oh, fine by me," she answered. "No need for a key, though. The door is not locked."

Stunned, Bryan could only stare at her. He couldn't form a sentence or even move. He'd never heard of someone who didn't lock their doors.

"What happened?" Becka asked him. "Why are you staring at me like that? Is there something on my face and I should know about?" she asked and touched her face to check for herself.

"You didn't lock your door," he said in a flat tone, which clearly conveyed how foolish he believed that to be.

"No, I didn't. Why should I?" Becka asked baffled both by the suggestion and his reaction.

"Why should you?" he asked in disbelief, then repeated more forcefully. "Why should you?"

"No need to get so upset over such a little thing," she patted his shoulder and continued in a tone meant to calm him down. "Believe me, there's no need to lock the door," the woman reassured him.

"Are you for real?" he burst out. "This is not a small village where everybody knows everybody, Becka. Even in small villages things happen. We're in a big city, for God's sake!" he finished his speech almost shouting. "People lock their doors, Becka."

"Come on, Bryan. What's the worst that could happen? You know what's meant to happen, it will," she said wisely.

"Spare me that bullshit. Don't go quoting shit to me!" he replied angrily. "You have to be more careful and start locking the damn door!"

Furious with her foolishness, Bryan kicked the door open with his foot as if he wanted to emphasize his statement.

Becka looked at him in silence, unsure of what to say, seeing how worked up he'd gotten. She thought to diffuse the tension and spoke calmly, hoping that that would make him calm down as well.

"Are you upset because I said what I said or is it because you think something might happen to me?"

"What the hell do you think?" Bryan barked again. "If you start locking the damn door and you're more careful from now on, you can quote me as much crap as you wish and whenever you feel like it!" Bryan snapped at her.

"Okay..." Becka dragged the word out. "So, you're saying you're concerned about me?"

"What kind of question is that, Becka? Of course, I'm concerned. What's wrong with you, woman?" he inquired with a grown and frowned at her.

"Nothing, nothing...," she said quickly to take his mind off his anger. "By the way, you might get tired holding me, Bryan. I'm not so light. So, either you put me down if you want to continue the conversation on the stairs or we could go inside... It's your choice, really," she said while looking at him, as if completely glossing over his mood.

Bryan felt frozen in place as if he couldn't believe her levity. He shook his head, closed his eyes in defeat before the strangest woman he'd ever come across, and then, carried her inside the house, closing the door with his foot.

Once inside, he looked at her questioningly, waiting for her directions.

"I suppose we could go to the kitchen first and have a cup of coffee," she answered his silent question. "I'm dying for a cup of coffee after the morning I've had," she groaned and continued, "I understand you don't feel like letting me stand so... The kitchen is right ahead, through the living room. It's the last door on the right," she pointed.

Bryan nodded curtly and carried her to the kitchen where he put her on a padded chair in her breakfast nook, which overlooked the garden. The entire wall to the garden was an expanse of glass framed by yellow curtains bound with thin silk ribbons.

Her garden sported an explosion of colors. Patches of all sorts of flowers bathed in the morning sunlight. They were plainly joyful and full of cheer.

At first sight, Bryan had the feeling that a madman had designed that garden. It was the oddest garden he'd ever seen. He couldn't remember to have ever seen so many colors and such undefined shapes in a garden.

His mother's garden displayed perfectly rectangular flowerbeds of petunias or roses, each with a well-defined spot for itself.

That strict setting was a far cry from Becka's otherworldly garden. It was nothing like those whirls of all sorts of flowers, tumbling off the pots, scattered throughout, without a distinguishable order to them. Many of the specimens were probably wild flowers because he hadn't ever seen them in a garden before.

He shook his head in disbelief at first, but after a few moments he finally understood that that garden was Becka entirely. It was wild, unpredictable, with sudden moods and unexpected surprises.

"So, what do you think of my garden?" he heard her soft voice from behind.

Turning around, he saw her standing a few steps behind him with an expectant light in her eyes. Despite her curiosity about his opinion, the glimmer in her chocolate gaze told him how attached she was to her garden.

"I think it suits you," he answered honestly. "It's exactly like you, Becka."

"Don't you think it's just crazy and I should change it, maybe tame it a little?" she asked, never taking her eyes off him.

He wouldn't have been the first to find the disorder of her little garden unsettling.

"What for? It's exactly how it should be, I think," Bryan answered her with a shrug of his shoulders. "I don't think you should change anything, baby. It really suits you," he said, stroking the side of her face with his thumb.

She beamed at him with happiness. Becka was pleased that he saw her garden the same way she did. She squeezed his hand appreciatively, before she turned to the kitchen counter where she started to prepare the coffee.

"I suppose you'd like to have a cup of coffee with me," she asked him while she was busying herself with the cups and saucers.

"Yeah, I'd like a cup of coffee," he replied, watching her small hands arrange the cups and saucers on a tray. "Becka, who told you, you should change your garden?" he asked curiously.

Becka shrugged it off as inconsequential, but answered his question to satisfy his curiosity. She remembered well they'd decided to get to know each other better, after all, even if it was about such small matters.

"Well, actually, everybody but you. At least my sister Ariel is a real pest about that garden. She has a knack for gardening and she thinks I should take every piece of advice she has in stock for me when it comes to it. She doesn't understand that I want to express myself, not some rule book. I don't want a geometrical garden with straight rows of flowers and individual flowerbeds... Anyway, that's a sore subject between the two of us, so I prefer to avoid it."

The man came up behind her, slipped his arms around her, and pulled her gently to him.

"You're a smart girl, Becka. You shouldn't change for anybody," he said, kissing the crown of her head first, then resting his head on the top of hers.

They stayed like that for a few moments that stretched on in silence. None of them wanted to pull away and end it.

Becka felt content in his embrace, as if she'd always belonged in those strong arms, which had carried her all the way to the house and inside. She wondered if she could make him stay and give her more time to discover the contradictory man hiding behind those sometimes-abrasive words, but who, in truth, was generous in his gestures and made her feel contented and cherished.

The shrill of the coffee maker startled them apart and both burst into laughter at their silly reaction.

"Well, it seems we both spaced out," Bryan tried to joke, but the humor didn't reach the serious, longing gaze he kept trained on her, as if he didn't want to let that moment end.

She smiled at him, her thoughts still on the comfortable, dreamlike embrace, but finally pushed him away, "Go and sit down. I'll bring the tray to the table."

"No, you go and sit down and I'll bring it to the table," he refused, giving her a little nudge to make her move. "You've just run the better part of a marathon, Becka, and you need to rest. Do you still feel up for going on the lake today?" he asked, worried about the intense workout she'd had that morning.

The woman nodded and went to the table, enjoying the fact that he didn't expect her to wait on him. She could still feel his eyes on her and wondered what he actually saw, if he liked the way she moved or how she looked.

Realizing the path of her thoughts, she admonished herself and almost shook her head. She never considered herself a simpleton who put a lot of stock on her looks. She wanted to be liked for more than that, but had to admit that there was some vanity there, inside her, which inspired a need to be appreciated for her appearance as well, and not only at an intellectual level.

The distant sound of Bryan's words snapped her out of her daydreaming and she realized she'd nearly missed what he was asking.

"Do you take your coffee with sugar and milk, Becka?"

"Oh, yes, I forgot to put the sugar bowl and the milk on the tray," she jumped out of her chair, ready to go back and correct her mistake, but he stopped her with a gesture.

"No need to bother yourself with that. Just tell me where you keep the sugar and milk and I'll take care of that," Bryan assured her.

"The sugar dish is in the cupboard above the coffee maker and the milk is in a little spout in the fridge," she told him, happy to sit tight and let him serve her.

Becka couldn't stop thinking, happily so, about his concern for her well-being and his willingness to make coffee in her home. It made a smile tug at her lips every time she thought of it.

Bryan opened the cupboard and took the sugar dish out. He examined it for a moment and noticed how small and delicate it was, a white piece of thin porcelain with small, dainty, blue flowers painted here and there, so lifelike that they seemed almost real, yet almost a blur at the same time, much like an illusion. He shook his head imperceptibly.

Taking out the milk spout from the fridge, he discerned the same delicate and thin porcelain and the same painted motif, which made him smile.

He had the feeling he'd uncovered another side of Becka that seemed to lean towards the fragile and artistic in her dishes. He'd already seen the lacy rims and the motif of little fairies dancing on the coffee cups and saucers, with their veils flying in the wind.

Bryan liked that side of her. As a matter of fact, he hadn't found anything he didn't like about her. Even her moods were refreshing.

The wild garden couldn't be more at odds with the elegant tea sets in her cupboard, but he couldn't help but feel that the contradiction was perfect for Becka, who wouldn't fit in one category alone. She was a free spirit, ready to express her opinions and didn't let anyone intimidate her, or at least she didn't let him intimidate her and that said something. He had a real talent to intimidate women.

Becka was fresh and young, but she wasn't rambling on and on about irrelevant things, which just made him feel old and left behind or which would put him to sleep. He'd been afraid she would bore him to tears the other evening and he'd been surprised when it didn't happen.

She'd been so lively and interesting that he hadn't wanted the evening to end. He only regretted he'd had to let her go inside her house and close the door behind her when he saw her to her house the night before.

The man loved she didn't try to pass for a fairy, just nibbling on some green leaves, enough not to lose consciousness. She wasn't obsessed with reaching the size dictated by the fashion of the time and that was something. He'd encountered that rare quality only in some women past sixty.

All the others were determined to be a size two and they were doing everything they could to get there, including starving to death.

He couldn't understand what was wrong with a size six or even eight or twelve. It wasn't as if the size had mattered. What was inside the package was more important.

He eyed Becka and appraised her to be a size ten, but that meant only she was the way the nature intended. She was gracious but with curves in the right places, especially in the areas he appreciated most.

Bryan had been drawn to her appearance at first, but now he kept discovering new things and his attraction to her deepened. He liked the Becka who was inclined to the fantastic and used the *Jaws* theme as a doorbell, but he also liked the Becka who created a garden out of a fairy tale.

The man brought the tray to the table where he placed it in front of her. He let his fingers brush a strand of hair away from her face, then he sat down, too.

"I was thinking I'd take a shower after we drink the coffee and then we could leave for our sailing adventure. What do you think?" she asked, smiling at him in excitement and poured the coffee in her whimsical cups.

"Works for me," he shrugged.

After a few moments of comfortable silence, he asked, "Where did you have to go this morning?"

She waved it off as unimportant at first, but then realised it was important for him and decided to tell him the truth.

"I told you I have some cousins … Well, my cousin Jay is a sort of a… gambler, you could say," Becka said hesitantly. "Last night he got involved in a game with some shady guys and apparently, they thought he was cheating and they roughened him up."

Bryan looked at her in disbelief.

"It's not like that," she specified seeing his thoughts reflected in his eyes. "Jay doesn't cheat but he has a... certain talent, let's say," she explained with wide gestures.

"What kind of ... talent?" Bryan asked her staring at her intently.

"Well... he knows what cards the opponent has in his hand," Becka rushed with the explanation, hoping she wouldn't have to say more than she was prepared to reveal.

"So, he's counting the cards...," Bryan started to say, but she interrupted him with a shake of her head.

"No?"

"No," she answered.

"Then what?"

She hesitated for a few moments, then replied uneasily, "He just knows what cards you have in your hand. Just never play with him. He doesn't cheat, but ... you wouldn't stand a chance."

"It's not possible, Becka," Bryan retorted. "Either he counts cards or he cheats."

She shook her head vigorously again.

"No, he doesn't. I'm sorry, it's not really for me to say, but just don't play with him, okay?"

Bryan shrugged, convinced she didn't want to admit her cousin was a cheater, who got beat up for it.

"So, you went to take care of him or what?" he asked, sampling his coffee.

"Well, when I got there around 3 a.m., he was in pretty bad shape and didn't want to go to the hospital... God, he hates hospitals more than I do."

"So, you played Florence Nightingale for him or what?"

She nodded and poured some more coffee in her cup, adding plenty of milk and sugar, which made Bryan smile. It wasn't coffee anymore. It looked more like milk with a touch of coffee.

"So, you slept only a few hours last night," the man concluded.

Becka nodded, but rushed to say, "Don't worry, Bryan, I still want to go on the lake. Maybe I'll sleep a little on the deck... Who knows?" she shrugged.

Bryan didn't say anything for a while. He sipped his coffee, watching her and assessing the shadows under her eyes.

"We can go out on the lake some other time, Becka, if you don't feel well enough. It's enough for me to see that you want to go."

"No, no, no," she jumped up from her seat. "No way! You promised we'd go today," she shouted at him.

"Easy, love, easy! Of course, we'll go if you want to. I was thinking you looked too tired...," Bryan said but stopped when he saw her shake her head. "We're going, we're going. Go take your shower and then we'll go," he rushed to mollify her.

Becka enthusiastically kissed his lips and rushed out of the room only to be stopped by his question.

"Becka, do you have a travel mug or something? Your coffee's great, and I think we could use a batch with us."

"Oh, yeah, there's one, I think... You know what, you check those cupboards there," she pointed to a row of cupboards, "and you might have a chance at finding it. When I get back, I could prepare some food to take with us," she told him joyfully.

"No need, Becka," he shook his head. "I've already taken care of the food. I told you we'd have a picnic on the lake so I have everything we need in my trunk."

"All right, then. You take care of the coffee and I will go shower. See you in ten minutes?" she said and he could hear the joy in her voice.

He started laughing heartily.

"What's so funny?" Becka asked.

"You're funny, Becka. Ten minutes? Come on. I've never seen a woman ready to leave the house in ten minutes and you still have to shower."

"Yeah? All right, let's make a bet," she challenged him, putting her hands on her hips.

He grinned and accepted her challenge.

"So, you like to bet even when it's not smart to do it?"

"You'll see, mister," she scoffed. "I bet you ten bucks that I'm back here in ten minutes, ready to go."

He stared at her, thinking the joke had gone
on long enough, but saw the mutinous expression
on her face and found himself nodding.

"You have a bet, Becka, then. Now, go, scat,"
Bryan push her along and smiled seeing her
fleeing the room as fast as she could.

CHAPTER FOUR

Bryan steered the yacht carefully with an eye out on the lake, where lots of sails crowded the horizon. He wanted to avoid any problems and close calls due to inattention.

He kept his other eye on Becka, who was sleeping soundly under the canopy he had mounted on the deck that morning for her before setting sail.

A gentle breeze soothed his warm skin. The sun was high in the sky and the air was hot. Now and then, the echo of a shout or a laughter over the water reached his ears. Otherwise, everything was silent. He felt wrapped in another world, all by himself. He enjoyed it every time he went out on the lake.

When they left the harbour, they worked together, although he didn't need anyone's help to sail his small yacht. Yet, he found out that he enjoyed working in a team with Becka, whose enthusiasm was contagious.

The woman knew her boats and she wasn't afraid to get a bit dirty and use her muscles. She might have been small, but she was a bolt of energy.

Bryan admired her knowledge about sailing and navigation, but more so her determination not to let her small size stand in her way. For such a slip of a girl, she had enough strength in her arms. Even though she was tired because of what had happened earlier that morning, she was still energetic enough to work shoulder to shoulder with him before falling asleep under the shade he'd created for her.

They'd been sailing for about two hours already and his mind was still on the bet he'd lost to Becka. Anyway, it wasn't like he had too much to do while she was sleeping. Minding the yacht wasn't too big a deal since he knew the drills by heart and could drive the boat and let his mind wander somewhere else at the same time.

That bet was bothering him and not because he'd lost money to Becka. The amount was ridiculous, even though Becka had jumped up and down with glee when she took the money from him. The thought made him smile again. It was a moment Bryan had enjoyed immensely.

The man couldn't explain why, but he felt a certain sense of fulfillment whenever he knew he was the reason behind that beaming smile on her face. It was as if her joy had been his own and he felt the need to give her more reasons to enjoy herself.

What puzzled him though was the fact he'd never seen a woman getting ready to go out under ten minutes flat, even if it was only about going sailing, rather than clubbing or something else.

Women, in his experience, needed much more time before setting foot out of the house. He'd had his share of waiting over the years and, of course, his share of the frustration that came with that.

To his astonishment, Becka hadn't even needed the full ten minutes she'd requested. She'd needed precisely eight minutes. Bryan had timed her, and how stupid did that seem now? In exactly eight minutes, she'd already been downstairs, ready to go.

Her hair was still wet from her shower. That was true. Becka had only taken the time to pass a comb through the thick locks of hair in a rush and she'd put on a pair of khakis and a t-shirt. That was the sum of her efforts. She hadn't wasted a second of those pesky eight minutes.

Bryan was bewildered. The young woman had the gift of continuously surprising him and he was sure she would still surprise him in his old age even if he'd spent a lifetime with her.

Becka was a bundle of contradictions. Altogether, she was shy and daring, whimsy and realistic, with a penchant for the horror, while living a fairy-tale in her eccentric garden with shapeless flowerbeds and the explosion of colors and wild flowers.

He kept discovering new things about her and everything made him shake his head in wonder. There were layers over layers still to be discovered and he hoped to have the time of his life to do just that.

Bryan was overjoyed he'd been so lucky to have her stumble over him and pour that hot coffee all over his shirt. It had been a chance he wouldn't get more than once. He wasn't afraid to admit it to himself, despite the tinge of desperation he felt crawl into his heart, because he lived with the constant fear she would disappear one day and his life would go back to what it had been before he met her. It saddened him. He knew his life would be bleak again and he didn't even know if he could go on as he'd done before, whenever things occurred and changed his path.

It was one thing when he didn't know what he was missing, and another to have a great thing in his life and lose it. He was sure he wouldn't be able to forget her the same way he'd forgotten the string of women before her.

In less than twenty-four hours, Becka had touched him like no one before and that was scary. Bryan was a realist and he couldn't discount the possibility that something so good wouldn't last forever.

Bryan was deep in his thoughts, but he still paid attention to Becka's every movement. He just couldn't take his eyes off her for very long, so he noticed when she woke up.

She rubbed her eyes like a child and the gesture made him grin. The woman looked very innocent and young. She hadn't put any make up on and there were no smudges under her eyes. He liked that. He dreaded seeing smudges under women's eyes in the morning.

Becka's hair stuck out in every direction and she looked like a porcupine. Bryan had to stifle his laughter, afraid she might misinterpret his amusement. She was very young and very touchy.

The man slowed the yacht down and kept his eyes always trained on her. He saw her look around with a faraway look on her face. She didn't know where she was and she was taking her bearings.

He noted when she finally took everything in and became aware of her surroundings, understanding sinking in. Then, she turned to look for him. When she saw him, her face lit up, as if she'd been truly happy to lay eyes on him.

That happy smile on her lips touched him profoundly. It was completely unexpected. It squeezed his heart and made him hope for impossible things.

Bryan believed she liked to be with him, at least for a while. She acted that way. Yet, he hadn't even dared to hope she would beam at him with so much joy just because he was still there. The contentment her gesture gave him winded him like a punch in the gut.

He wanted to say something, to let her know how much everything meant to him, but words couldn't pass the knot in his throat. Had he been a lesser man, he'd have cried of joy, and that would have spoiled everything. No woman could stand a man crying, no matter what she said. And why the hell would he feel like that? He gave himself a stern nudge to put himself back together.

"You have a good sleep, Becka?"

Becka stood up with a nod and walked over to him with a dreamy light in her eyes. He watched her lazy stride and admired her long unclad legs covering the spread of the deck.

When they got on the yacht, she'd taken off her capris and t-shirt and was left with only a two-piece bathing suit on. Bryan couldn't stop himself from noticing again how the bathing suit hugged her curves enticingly. He felt his pants tighten a little more.

She wasn't tall by any means. She reached only to his chest and that with her shoes on. Despite her height, her legs were long and her ankles were supple and gracious, even though her thighs were not on the thin side.

In Bryan's opinion, she couldn't complain about anything. The entire package was there and it was tempting like hell for a man who lost more ground every minute.

Becka stopped next to him and leaned on him. She slipped one arm around him and let her head fall on his chest with an easy gesture as if she'd been doing it for ages.

Bryan looked at the crown of her head for a few moments and then, he brushed some of the strands around, trying to bring some order to her dishevelled hair. He abandoned her tousled hair and raised her chin with his thumb. He looked at her for a couple of seconds and then, he leaned down to kiss her.

He lingered for a few moments, just a hair away from her lips. He wanted to give himself the time to inhale that sweet and fresh scent, which was definitely Becka's.

It was only after a few moments of panting expectation that Bryan took her mouth into a searing kiss. The man put into that kiss all the longing, churning inside him for the last two hours, while he'd been watching her sleep there in the nest he'd made for her on deck, and thinking of how it would feel to have her in his arms and know that she belonged only to him.

When Bryan raised his head, and looked down at her, her eyes were still closed. Becka was still clinging to his arms as if she couldn't find her balance.

Her mouth was rosy and her lips were slightly swollen and satisfaction welled up in his chest. It was gratifying for Bryan to see he had such an effect on her because, he had to admit it, the little woman held his thoughts and heart in her little fist.

Her mouth still beckoned to him, and he found himself unable to refuse it. Bryan leaned in again and brushed his mouth over hers flittingly. Then, he bit her bottom lip lightly and made her moan, which increased his desire a notch. His mind was already racing ahead, thinking about taking her right there on the deck, when he heard her whisper.

"I'm hungry, Bryan."

Her words were like a blow to the head. The man just blinked and stared at her. Becka didn't even open her eyes and her fingers were still digging into his arms. Bryan was fired up like a rocket, and Becka seemed oblivious to everything. He shook his head as if he couldn't believe her.

"Are you sure?" Bryan asked her, squeezing her hip, unaware his fingers were digging strongly in the soft curve and could have marked her.

His actions made her nose twitch and she opened her eyes wide. Her mouth formed a perfect 'o' and just looked at him for a few seconds. Becka seemed unable to say anything, but she regained her gumption soon enough.

"I said I'm hungry, and that means I'm pretty sure, Bryan," she scowled at him.

"We were just kissing, Becka…" Bryan started to say with reproach, but she interrupted him, pressing a gentle finger to his lips.

"So? Can't I kiss you and be hungry at the same time? Or everything must be on a specific timetable with you?" she raised her voice a little, which made him look at her with stunned eyes.

"Wow, that's a good way to ruin romance, baby," Bryan chastised her.

He was hurt because he had hoped she would feel the same way as him and her reaction was like a cold shower over his feelings.

Becka shrugged with indifference and finally let go of his arms. She stepped back and looked him straight in the eyes.

"Romance is great, Bryan, even for me, but I can feel romance even if I eat, you know," she replied with practicality.

"Okay, Becka, hold your horses, we'll eat soon enough," Bryan conceded with resignation.

He put aside his dreams of a little lovemaking on the deck. Becka was full of surprises and he needed to adjust his thinking to her if he wanted their relationship to survive, and he did.

"Soon? Why not now? I'm hungry now, you know," she insisted with defiance in her voice.

"Because I was thinking of sailing over there," he explained patiently and pointed to an island not far away. "I was thinking we could have our picnic on the shore of that island, Becka. I'm sure you'd like to eat there instead of here on the deck," he continued drily. "I know I would," he muttered under his breath.

Becka looked toward the island, shading her eyes from the sun with her hand. Then, she looked at the covered portion of the deck with indecision.

"It's tempting, I won't say no," she murmured, turning back to him, "but you won't be able to moor there, so that point is moot," she said louder. "So, we can eat here, even though it is not so idyllic," she concluded, all too eager to eat. She hadn't eaten since the night before and she'd already used up a lot of her energy.

"Not really," Bryan said, still steering the yacht full speed to the island. "There's a dock there and I can moor my boat just fine."

His voice was always dry and that was a sign he was just a bit pissed off with all that fuss. He understood Becka hadn't had breakfast and she'd already made a lot of effort that morning, but he was sure she wouldn't die if she'd waited for a few more minutes.

The woman shrugged again. That seemed to be one of her habits, and one he found very endearing. Then, she went to sit on the bench near the steering wheel, watching the horizon.

"Are you upset or something?" Bryan asked a little unsettled by her sudden change of mood.

He didn't deal very well with women's moods and he would usually try to get out of the line of fire when something like that happened. However, this time, he felt compelled to understand where everything went wrong. He had invested a lot of himself in that fragile relationship and didn't want to let it go to waste.

"No, why do you ask?" Becka asked, fussing around with the blanket on the bench.

She pretended she was busy folding it so she could avoid his eyes.

"I don't know," Bryan replied matter-of-factly. "It's like you're upset. You're not happy like you were earlier and you seem in a mood. You raised your voice," he pointed out.

Becka looked at him shocked. She had no reply for a few seconds but then she retorted, "I'm not in a mood."

Bryan didn't say anything back. He thought he'd better give her some space, hoping she'd be her usual self again after a while.

"All right," she jumped off the bench upset. "Now you know!" she cried out throwing her arms in the air dramatically, and stomping toward the other side of the yacht out of his line of sight.

Bryan looked after her bewildered. He even craned forward to see her better and only after a few moments dared to ask, "Know what?"

Becka came back with small and hesitant steps, her hands knotted behind her and her head down. She was biting her lower lip, preoccupied with how to formulate her answer.

"I'm not at my best when I wake up, Bryan. You need to give me a little space for a few minutes, and then everything's fine again," she confessed with a small voice as if she had admitted to a capital sin.

Bryan grinned, relieved there was nothing else the matter and he had worried for nothing after all. He reached out to Becka to pull her to him.

"Come on, baby, that's not such a big deal. As long as I know that, I can cope with it and I can give you all the space you need."

She took his hand and came closer to him.

"I know I'm a porcupine whenever I wake up, Bryan. It's not like I want to be, you know, but… that's how I am."

"In more ways than one," Bryan said under his breath, but she heard him and looked up at him with a frown.

"What do you mean?"

He tried to avoid saying anything more. He didn't want to aggravate her more than he had already done it, but her eyes were trained on him and demanded an answer.

The man fidgeted for a few moments, trying to buy some more time so he could come up with something less offensive, but there was no way out of it, so he decided to tell her the truth.

"Your hair," he waved around her head. "It looks like… you're a porcupine," he finally expressed his thoughts.

Becka gasped in distress and both of her hands shot up at her hair to tame it, but to no avail.

"Damn it, I shouldn't have skipped the conditioner this morning," she wailed.

Bryan laughed when he heard her dramatic wail. Becka did like her drama and that should have turned him off. Instead, he found her more and more loveable with every moment and that seemed odd.

That wasn't him, the one from before he had met her and that was disquieting. He shook his head and abandoned that train of thought afraid of the conclusion he might reach.

"So, if I understand correctly, you skipped using your conditioner so you could be downstairs on time?" he remarked and not without malice.

"Okay, laugh as much as you want," she retorted fisting her hands on her hips. "I wasn't sure I'd be ready in ten minutes, I admit. The conditioner takes about three minutes to apply," she snapped, and began patting her mane of wild hair in an attempt to tame it.

"Yeah, you'd have been a minute late, that's true," Bryan replied, always smiling. "Would that have been so bad?" he inquired.

For a moment, Becka stopped her frenzy movements and looked up at him. After a couple of seconds, she replied with serious eyes. "Yes,

Bryan, very bad. I don't like to lose..." she wrinkled her nose. Then she thought to add, "I think you'd better learn now I'm a sore loser, Bryan... Still want to have that picnic with me?" she inquired in a small voice.

Bryan reached for her again and pulled her into a bear hug, making her gasp in surprise. He didn't let her go, but gathered her tighter to him and whispered in her hair.

"You're perfect, Becka, just perfect. Of course, I want to picnic with you, baby," he continued, touching his head of hers. He inhaled the fresh scent of her hair and felt content to let the moment flow.

Becka could hardly breathe though. Bryan didn't seem to know his strength and his hug was very tight. Yet, Becka started smiling in the folds of his shirt, happy because he wasn't put out by her mood or by her confession.

Bryan held her for a few more moments before he found the strength to let her go and return to the helm. She welcomed the reprieve and filled her lungs with fresh air.

"In a few minutes, we'll be there, Becka," he said and pointed toward the dock that now appeared to be very close.

Becka looked over the expanse of water and saw that they were headed toward a dock which appeared in a very good shape. From what she could see, someone had taken good care of it. It wasn't one of the docks left there to rot in the sun and under the rains.

"I think that dock belongs to someone, Bryan. Won't they complain if we moor there?" she glanced at him and inquired.

He waved her concern away and explained the dock belonged to a friend of his, who let him use it whenever he wanted.

"The best part is, he's not even here, so we have the place to ourselves. No one will bother us for the entire day."

He kept paying attention to his driving as the shore was near now.

"He also let me use his house now and then, so if you have enough of the sun and the lake, we can go there and sit on the porch or even go inside and lie down on a bed."

Becka looked at him with doubt in her eyes, but shrugged. She decided to let him entertain his illusions. She didn't enjoy ruining anyone's hopes, yet, she was sure no one would be so generous and let their friend come and go at their will.

She was close enough to her cousins, but she didn't think any of them would welcome her in their house whenever she wanted if they weren't there as well. She was pretty sure they would frown upon her bringing a friend with her and inviting him into their bed.

"Should I get dressed, you think?" Becka asked. She didn't know what to expect once they got off the boat.

Bryan shook his head. He reassured her that they were alone there, and she didn't need to fear they would meet anyone.

He slowed down when he approached the mooring and handled the boat with a professional's ease, which made Becka beam with pride. That, he liked. He liked to see she found pride in what he did, even though it was something as insignificant as mooring the boat.

Bryan enjoyed basking in her attitude toward him. He even cherished the moments when she got angry with him because, in his mind, it meant she took the time to see him, the man, however strange that sounded even in his ears.

CHAPTER FIVE

Bryan helped Becka off the boat, balancing the food basket and a small cooler in his other hand. It wasn't a small basket by any means and Becka's thoughts started racing when she saw it. She was trying to guess what delicious things he had hidden in there.

Becka couldn't wait to partake in the picnic he had prepared. She also wondered why Bryan wouldn't let her help him carry anything. From the look of things, he had too many things to take care of at the same time.

The man had even draped a blanket over his shoulder and with the other hand on the small of her back, he guided her towards a cluster of trees a short distance from the shore.

"I remember there's a nice meadow there, right in front of those trees," he explained to her. "It's a good area for a picnic, Becka, you'll see. We can see the lake from there and if I remember correctly, you like watching the boats, although not many sail past here, I must tell you. This island is quite secluded. It's not in the way of traffic. We'll also have cover from the sun. Those trees over there," he took his hand off the small of her back and pointed in the distance, "make for a great shade. I think it's a perfect spot for our picnic. And later, if you don't want to go to the house, we can stretch out on this blanket and no one will be the wiser," he prattled on.

Becka listened to him and smiled. She couldn't help but wonder why he was talking so much. He didn't look like the type to chatter at length about insignificant little things. He seemed somewhat nervous, and she couldn't understand why.

She suspected something wasn't what seemed to be. Yet, she didn't feel she was in any kind of danger, so she pushed the thought aside.

Bryan didn't let her help him with laying down the blanket or arranging the food either. He just directed her to lie down under the shadow of a tree and wait for him to prepare everything.

Once he started unwrapping the food, her taste buds went in overdrive. The smell of the juicy chicken surrounded by a mound of French fries made her mouth water and she sighed with anticipated pleasure. The Caesar salad, coming out of the basket afterwards, looked tasty as well, but didn't hold a candle to the casserole of homemade chicken with fries covered by grated cheese. The man had overdone himself.

Bryan laughed when she licked her lips, while eyeing the food with excitement.

"Come on, let's dig in, sweetie, and keep in mind, I also have dessert and you definitely need to save some space for it. You'll love it, Becka, I promise you," he said and reached out to her.

Becka sat on the blanket and playfully slapped his arm. Then, she reached for one of the plastic plates he had put next to the basket on the blanket. She topped the plate with chicken and fries. She'd just finished filling the plate up when he also uncovered a container with Greek salad, which was her favorite. She forgot about the Caesar salad instantly.

"Oh. I haven't left any space for that on my plate and I want some," she pouted in disappointment, eyeing the salad, which was beaconing at her.

"Don't worry, we can both eat directly from here, can't we?" he reassured her and put the container between them.

He crossed his legs, copying her stance and spooned some of the chicken casserole on his plate.

Becka nodded and attacked the food with fervour. The aromas had made her hunger rise to new levels. Bryan took a moment or two to watch her eat, then, with a smug smile on his lips, he dug into his food, as well.

"Do you cook?" she asked, tasting the chicken flavored with butter, lemon and some herbs she didn't even bother to identify.

The taste was exquisite and that was all that mattered. She was very curious where he had found it but she decided to go with her first guess. He must have made it.

"Yes, I do. I had to learn how to cook since I like to eat and I got sick of so much take-out," he replied with a nod. Then, he asked her, "Do you like it?"

"Oh, it's great. Amazing even... I can't cook, Bryan," she suddenly said with regret.

Bryan glanced at her a little taken aback by her sudden confession. She was indeed upset with her admission. That genuine disappointment with something so unimportant made him smile.

He stroked her arm and comforted her, "It's not a problem, Becka. You probably can do other things. It's not like I'd want you in front of the stove cooking away…," he said and let the words linger between them. "I want you somewhere else anyway," he mumbled, but her keen hearing didn't fail her this time either, and Becka burst into laughter, light-heartedly slapping his arm again.

"You're a naughty boy, Bryan," she managed to say through peals of laughter.

Bryan glanced at her and decided to try his luck, "Naughty, naughty, but are you against what I'm thinking?"

She looked at him for a few moments, seeming to consider his question and finally she shook her head. A faint blush spread over her face and made him grin. He liked to see her blush. Her innocence was refreshing and made him feel manlier, which he didn't mind at all.

After a little pause, the conversation tittered around insignificant things with long stretches of silence. That didn't bother them. They felt comfortable enough together and didn't need to fill the quietness with meaningless chatter.

Being together, sharing the good food and enjoying the air of the lake was enough for both of them. They enjoyed each other's company and that was what mattered.

The day was growing hotter, but the shadow of the trees offered them a respite from the hot air. The infrequent breeze cooled them even more.

In the distance, the sails of the boats spotted the surface of the lake, but the noise of the town didn't reach them. They had the feeling they were secluded in their own paradise, just the two of them, free to talk about anything and everything, free to kiss each other, whenever the mood struck, or to feed each other pieces of succulent chicken now and then, bursting into laughter when one of them would drop some food.

Once they filled themselves with the main course, Bryan revealed two big slices of triple chocolate cake and Becka's eyes widened. She had a weakness for chocolate cake, especially when it came in three thick layers of chocolate. She attacked the cake with renewed gusto even though she was already full.

Becka had never been able to say no to chocolate cake. It was the curse of her life or at least one of them. She couldn't pass on such a delightful dessert and she expressed her appreciation for his taste in organizing picnics.

After a while, Bryan leaned back on the trunk of a tree, with her snuggled up tight in his arms, his chin resting on the top of her head.

Becka closed her eyes and, with a content sigh, she let herself drift into sleep once again, feeling safe in the strong arms wrapped tightly around her.

Bryan felt her chest rise and fall under his arms and her soft breathing lulled him to sleep as well, making him forget about the food left there on the blanket.

A black squirrel had been watching the feast spread out on the blanket for a while now. It was on a branch above their heads and, when it considered it was safe enough, because the humans were out for the count, it came down and stole a piece of the chicken and ran away with it. No one was the wiser.

***

Becka slept for about an hour and a half and woke up refreshed and ready to attack the world again. She realized she was still in Bryan's arms, and she turned her head to look up at him. He was already awake and met her eyes squarely.

The change in Becka's breathing had woken him up and he had been waiting to see what she wanted to do. He also remembered what had happened on the yacht earlier and he didn't want a repeat of the stupid quarrel they had.

All their squabbles seemed unsubstantial. Most of the time, they were the result of misunderstandings. He found them to be a waste of time and he'd proposed himself to avoid any quarrel if possible. The stakes were too high for him and he didn't want to miss on the chance he had been given when he met her.

Becka raised her arm and touched his face with hesitant fingers. She let them skim over the beard shadowing his face, and touched his scar fleetingly. She felt him tense for a second, but when her fingers continued to trace the contour of his face, he relaxed. Then, she turned in his arms and faced him on her knees.

Both watched each other intently. No words were exchanged. Becka leaned in slightly and put her hands on his chest. From there, her fingers started exploring the hard planes beneath.

Bryan left his hands rest on her hips and waited to see what she had in mind, although her wandering fingers had a maddening effect on his system. He could feel the fire stoking inside him.

Hesitantly, Becka leaned forward and pressed her lips to his for a brief kiss and looked up at him afterwards. He was looking down at her, his eyes half covered by his lashes.

She decided to be more forward and kissed him again. This time, her tongue traced the contour of his lips thoroughly, learning their taste and shape.

That spelled the end of her initiative. Bryan couldn't take it anymore and he pulled her forcibly into his arms to lower her on the blanket. He covered her body with his and kissed her with all the longing he had gathered in his heart since the day before.

It was the first time he'd ever felt so much excited at the thought of holding a woman in his arms and so impatient to have her. Not even as a teenager, had he ever been so edgy at the idea of making love as he was now.

At first, Bryan tried to control himself and focused on exploring Becka's lips with his own. Only after he learnt their texture and felt them tremble, he moved on, and started exploring her entire mouth. His tongue slowly slid past her parted lips and danced against hers, filling himself with her unique flavor and texture.

Bryan took his time and tasted her leisurely. He wanted to enjoy every second and immerse himself in the pleasure she offered him.

His gestures were measured and slow, designed to entice and seduce. His calloused fingers stroked the side of her face and went up to mingle with her mane that still stuck out in a frenzy of honey.

Bryan pushed himself onto her hard and the shock of his move made her gasp, but the sound got lost in his voracious mouth.

Far from satisfied, he continued to make love to her lips while his hands started wandering along her neck and arms, leaving behind little shocks and shivers.

Bryan's caresses shook Becka to the core. She trembled against him and in one last lucid moment, Bryan raised his head and looked at her.

"If you don't want me to continue, say it now. I don't know if I'll be able to stop later, Becka," he admitted in a husky voice.

Becka nodded to let him know she wanted him to continue with that torture of her senses. Shyness shone in her eyes and tugged at his heart.

The young woman couldn't find the words to make her wishes known to him. Becka wasn't even sure if there were still words somewhere in her mind. She was immersed in a sea of sensations. Even if she wanted to say anything, her throat felt somewhat constricted and she couldn't utter a sound beside the moans that didn't even register in her ears.

Something odd was going on inside her body but it felt good, so Becka wanted him to continue touching her with all that incensed passion she could read in his eyes.

Bryan's eyes had lost that icy shine she had seen before. Now, an unusual light had lit and darkened those cold blue irises and she basked in that light. Becka felt proud of herself because she was responsible for putting that hot light in there.

Bryan stared at her a moment longer, to make sure she was all right with what was going to happen between the two of them, and then he gathered her into his arms.

He wanted to let her feel his strong desire for her and to let the tension, which had seized his body, sip into hers.

He kissed her lips again and nibbled on them a couple of times before he deepened the kiss some more to satisfy his overwhelming need to become one with her.

Becka wrapped her arms around his neck and welcomed the heat of his body. Her skin tingled and longed for his touches. When his teeth nibbled at the soft skin of her neck, she sighed and let go of any coherent thought.

She had completely forgotten they were outside in the open, lying on a blanket and, maybe, a boat might sail close enough, and people might see them. She was only aware of her strong desire to have that man fulfill all her fantasies and step with him into her womanhood.

She abandoned everything in Bryan's knowledgeable hands and let him mold her body with his touches.

Bryan took off the upper piece of her swimming suit and filled his hands with her full breasts. He held them for a few moments, shaping them with his fingers, and then, he rubbed his cheek on the soft skin of one of them.

Becka shivered when she felt the roughness of his beard on the sensitive spot. She arched, needing to feel him closer, and that encouraged him to be bolder. His tongue flicked out and licked at the little tip, which rose timidly into his touch. Bryan licked it slowly, teasingly, and she felt like her body was on fire. She moaned, closing her eyes. Satisfied with her response, he took her nipple into his mouth and started sucking on it hungrily, to fill himself with her scent and taste.

The first flick of his tongue triggered deep vibrations in her lower body. Her body was strung like a bow, and every fiber of her body was impatiently waiting for release.

The sensations were sharp and pleasantly painful. Her yearning increased tenfold. When he started sucking on her breast in earnest, she cried out keenly, unable to control the tautness bottled up inside her. All the sensations assaulting her senses were strong and overwhelming. She couldn't control them. She felt like she'd been thrust into the eye of a tornado.

Bryan let go of her breast and she breathed with relief. The tension became more bearable. It lasted only one moment though. He moved to the other breast, and the sweet agony started all over again.

Now, his fingers were playing with the little hyper-sensitized nipple he had already tormented with his mouth. He was rolling it between his fingers, now and then, pinching it and tugging at it suddenly.

Becka couldn't discern what happened to her anymore. She couldn't focus on a specific feeling. Her skin tingled all over, and the ocean of sensations in her lower belly had turned into a volatile storm, which shredded her to pieces. The intensity of her feelings was so high now that she was moaning constantly and she started writhing uncontrollably underneath him.

She didn't know whether she wanted Bryan to continue with his ministrations or she wanted him to stop so she could escape the multitude of bombarding feelings, which had turned her into a mass of sensations and erased all reasoning from her brain.

After he sucked at her breast until she was close to delirium, his lips started their journey down and his tongue flicked and swirled here and there, his teeth nibbling at her skin and sending piercing shivers through her entire body.

Becka laced her fingers in his hair to feel more of him. She also needed some support through the storm of sensations, ravaging her body.

When he dipped his tongue into her belly button, she almost jumped off the blanket. Immediately his fingers dug into her hips to keep her there, prisoner to everything he had to give her.

By now, Becka was lost completely in a sea of piercing and coiling sensations. Her eyes were closed. She moved under him unconsciously.

Her movement made it harder for him. It was difficult not to plunge in and take what he wanted the most.

When he reached the edge of her bikini, he lowered it slowly and lavished every uncovered inch of her skin with his passionate attention. His tongue was swirling over spots she had never thought sensitive before.

Becka let his hair go and propped herself up on her elbows. With wide, shocked eyes, she watched him attentively, biting her lips nervously. She didn't want him to stop, but she wasn't sure she wanted him to continue his journey south.

Bryan noticed her move. He thought she might back off then. Becka was excited. That was true. Yet, she was also new to all of that and she was teetering on the edge of uncertainty.

Bryan removed her bikini with a hasty move and, then, he looked up at her, questioning her intentions.

At first, she didn't say anything, but stared back at him. After a few seconds of hesitation, she nodded her agreement slightly only to receive a ruthless smile in return. That grin of his made her feel fearful and unsure of what was about to come.

It wasn't as if she hadn't known what was supposed to happen next. She had a general idea about how that worked but she didn't know what to expect exactly. What she knew was that she couldn't say '*no*' to Bryan.

Becka did want to make love to him. She'd already made her mind up the day before and her body had followed suit the moment Bryan kissed her that afternoon.

Bryan pushed her gently back onto the blanket and his head lowered over the intimate place he had just uncovered. When she felt that his face touched her thigh, and became aware that he was taking in her new and strong scent, Becka blushed violently.

She was happy he couldn't see her face. She was ashamed because she was behaving with such lack of sophistication but there were some things she just couldn't control.

Bryan's fingers hovered over her body for a few tense seconds. His hands slid up and down her thighs, in a slow and maddening movement, his searching fingers leaving newly awakened tingles in their wake, whenever they squeezed and stroked her muscles.

When he felt that her arousal augmented, he pushed her legs apart gently, and stroked the inside of her thighs, starting from the back of her knees and sliding up, excruciatingly slowly, until his fingers reached the top of her legs. There, he let his fingers slide over her womanhood like an illusion and she shivered again.

This time, the urgency of her need was much higher. Becka locked her fingers on the sides of his head, ready to pull him up to her.

Yet, he had something else in mind. Bryan didn't care for her intention of bringing him back to her mouth. He burrowed his nose in the one spot he had wanted to touch all day and breathed her scent deeply. His tongue followed and started making love with her and drive her crazy.

Becka was already teetering on the edge. She felt as if electrical shocks sensitized every nervous ending in her skin and the flickers of his tongue didn't make it easier at all.

Once more, Becka lost any conscious thought and she could only chant breathlessly, "Please, please, please!" over and over again.

She wasn't aware she was begging him. Becka didn't know if she wanted him to stop doing those maddening things to her because she couldn't take it anymore or if she wanted him to continue his arousing torment.

Becka had already reached a point where she could just feel. Thinking was something remote. Instinct and pleasure had already replaced reasoning and, somewhere in her subconscious level, she feared she was losing herself in that uncontrollable mass of emotions.

Whenever his talented tongue reached that sensitive nub, which his fingers had been caressing and rolling for a time that seemed a small eternity already, Becka felt small explosions everywhere inside her lower body.

Bryan's thumb stroked over that ball of sensory endings unexpectedly and, at the same time, he sucked at her already swollen little clit throwing her in an ocean of new sensations.

When the explosions inside her became all too violent, she cried out and her fingers pulled his hair. Her lower body rose completely off the blanket instinctively, seeking more of the attentions he lavished on her.

Bryan raised his head and glanced at her. At the same time, his thumb pressed her core. He was satisfied to see she had abandoned herself to the pleasure he could give her. With the same ruthless smile on his lips, he returned to the throbbing nub, which he stroked tenderly with his tongue, until she calmed down.

When he felt the tension had left her body, Bryan looked up at Becka's reddened face and quivering lips. He continued to touch her thighs and abdomen with long and appeasing strokes, his fingers massaging and burrowing gently in her skin here and there.

Bryan dipped his head once more, and his lips trailed up her body with feather-like kisses and nibbles at a few choice spots. He locked on one of her sensitive breasts with his lips and sucked it in his mouth, while his fingers played with the peak of the other.

She exhaled deeply and moaned. Her eyes opened wide at the shock of the new sensation. Bryan continued to feast on her breast for a while longer and made her arch her back to reach deeper in his mouth.

He sucked her nipple deeper and, at the same time, his fingers shaped her breast and pushed it higher to his mouth. After a few more moments, he released her nipple and a breeze of air on the wet and sensitized nipple made Becka shiver.

Bryan traced more kisses up her torso until his feverish lips reached her neck. There, he decided to make a halt for a few moments and play with her skin, which was already oversaturated with sensations.

She quivered again but he still continued with his sensual trail of kisses and nibbles up to her ear. When he licked the whorl of her ear, the knot inside her coiled again.

Becka turned her head to kiss him and she was startled when she tasted not only him but also herself on his lips. The mingled scents aroused her even more, even though she didn't think it would have been possible to feel anything more.

She kissed his lips at first and bravely nibbled at them as he had done to her, and rejoiced when she felt him quiver. Payback was only fair.

Becka stroked his strong arms and tried to learn the shape of his coiled muscles. She wrapped hers around him with a sense of possession she didn't know she had. A vixen smile formed on her lips and that uncharacteristic smile incited him to grin at her, as well.

Bryan took her mouth again in a scorching toe-curling kiss. He rubbed himself of her, enjoying the feel of her skin.

"Should I take my clothes off, sweetie?" he asked in a husky whisper.

"Yes, please," Becka moaned and patted his arm, more to encourage herself than him.

Bryan stood in a split-second and with hasty movements, he yanked his clothes off. He couldn't wait any longer. He couldn't take his eyes off her body.

Becka was stretched out on the blanket and she was waiting impatiently for him to touch her again. Her skin wore the marks of his beard and greedy fingers, and her lips were red and swollen from their passionate kisses.

Becka looked very well-loved, but he still wanted to give her much more and take his own pleasure at the same time. Bryan lowered himself onto the blanket and over her.

He braced himself on his left elbow and the fingers of his right hand skimmed over her silky skin. He dipped his head and his lips played with her mouth before trailing down to her neck where he marked her again with a mild bite. Her moan amplified his desire.

Bryan hadn't thought it was possible to want a woman more than he already did. Yet, desire knotted in his belly, making him ache at a new level. He was painfully hard and he needed her badly. He needed his release but didn't want to rush her.

His fingers closed on one of her breasts again, playing with it, ready to tease more, when she wrapped her arms around him and pulled him over her with a strength he didn't know she had. Bryan understood her quiet message to hurry and make love to her, yet he didn't want to steal anything from her first experience.

Determined to make her enjoy their lovemaking as much as he did, Bryan leaned forward and started to suck on her breast again, as his hand brushed down south and played with the little tense nub between her thighs.

"Now, Bryan, now!" she cried out. "I want you, now. Enough with all that torture," she demanded, at the same time pulling at his hair savagely.

Bryan laughed and hugged her, gathering her body to him. Then, he covered her, pushing her legs apart so she could cradle him. He kissed her lips with a tenderness that was in direct contrast with the wild kisses he had given her before.

"I've never been with a virgin, Becka, my sweetie, so, you're out of luck here," he whispered with regret over her lips. "I'll try to be gentle, but…"

"You're doing just fine," she whispered back, reassuringly, "but hurry now, Bryan. I need you now," she continued with a tense voice.

He laughed nervously and found his way inside her, raising her hips with his hands. He started pushing slowly forward because she was very tight, but Becka had lost all patience by then and pushed up with force to meet him, just to cry out when he was all the way in.

Becka felt he was stretching her beyond her limit. The pressure she experienced inside was painful and delightful at the same time.

"Are you all right?" Bryan asked with concern.

He was afraid she had been hurt because of the sudden invasion.

"Just perfect," she whispered and smiled at him. Her eyes were wide with wonder. "I'm pretty sure there should be much more than this," she said in a conspiring voice, and flexed her inner muscles.

Her reply prompted Bryan's laughter again, but the squeeze of her inner muscles turned the laughter into a growl.

"Yes, there is, baby, there is," Bryan said through clenched teeth.

Then, he started moving inside her more forcibly, making love to her in earnest.

Becka gasped when she felt him move inside her. He stretched her and the sensation was painful and agonizingly pleasant at the same time. She clung to his arms. She was afraid she would get lost in the storm of sensations.

Becka loved feeling his weight on her. She loved that he was a part of her. She might have had a twinge of pain for a few seconds, but that was soon forgotten.

She relished in the pressure and pleasure he was giving her with his body. Unconsciously, she started moving in rhythm with him. Pushing against him made her feel much more. The sensations were more intense.

She slid her fingers along his back to the top of his thighs and both of them gasped, even though for different reasons.

Bryan lifted one of her legs and wrapped it around his waist. He stroked her thigh from behind her knee up to the hip, using just the tip of his fingers and awakening nerve endings that had relaxed. His rough-skinned palm slid further and touched the roundness of her backside. Then, he pressed on her rump and brought her pelvis closer to his. The change in position ignited sparks through her veins and she felt the tension coiling inside her unbearably painful.

Now Bryan could push deeper and she had the feeling he was connected to her in ways she had never imagined possible. Bryan bowed his head and bit gently one of her nipples.

Becka cried out as her skin tingled everywhere. Then, Bryan pulled the nipple inside his mouth and sucked hard on it. The tautness inside her exploded and, for a moment, she felt pulled apart in a multitude of directions, only to uncoil into a sphere of sensations that set her skin on fire.

Becka cried out again and louder this time. Before she fell into the abyss of sensations and lost any coherent cognitive functions, Becka felt Bryan give in to the ultimate pleasure. She collapsed having the vague feeling that she heard him groan but it was something remote and uncertain.

Becka didn't know how long she had been out, but when she came back to the real world, she felt Bryan's lips brush along her neck tenderly. He was breathing hard and his hands were shaking, but he still took care of her and stroked her lovingly.

"Are you all right, baby?" he whispered in her ear, taking her earlobe between his lips and biting it delicately.

Becka shivered as the aftermath waves were still present, and his bite intensified them more. She tried to say *'yes'*, but she didn't seem to find her voice anymore. Her voice was lodged somewhere in her throat and she couldn't get any words out. She nodded and hugged him tighter.

Bryan rolled on his side with her nestled tightly in his arms and kissed the crown of her head. He covered her legs with one of his, unwilling to let go of her and pull away yet. He continued to stroke her back and her upper thighs, while rubbing his chin on the top of her head affectionately.

"Was it okay for you or...?" Bryan asked without even thinking about what he was going to say.

He didn't want to ask. He didn't want to hear it had been bad for her and he had behaved like a man who'd thought only of his pleasure and hadn't paid any attention to hers. He didn't want to hear the lie in her voice if she'd said *'yes'*, but she actually hadn't felt anything.

Bryan failed to understand his insecurity around Becka. It was probably because he wanted much more from her than he had ever wanted from another woman or because he had had the chance or bad luck, depending how she felt and what she thought, to be the first man who had made love to her.

Bryan, for one, couldn't complain. He had never been with a woman that had belonged only to him. He might have liked to think he was above such caveman's thoughts, but he had to admit it felt good to know he was the only man she had known in biblical terms.

Whatever the case, Bryan was beside himself with anger, especially because he knew his insecurity could ruin the best thing that had ever happened to him.

Becka kept silent and kissed his chest while her fingers brushed the curly coarse hair that peppered his skin. Then, she looked up at him with a dreamy expression in her eyes and nodded staring at him.

A smile started to flourish on her lips shyly and the sweetness of the moment hit him like a fist in his gut. Bryan pulled her tighter into his arms, making her protest.

"It's too tight, Bryan. I can't breathe," she said in a small voice.

Bryan became aware he had been too rough with her and loosened his hug to let her breathe. Yet, he didn't let go of her completely. He still needed to feel her body against his.

Actually, and that was quite astounding, he needed her again. Bryan even thought about the possibility of making love to her once more, but he decided against it. It had been her first time and he didn't want to hurt her. He could have her tomorrow again if she wanted, too.

They remained entwined, both content to be close one to the other and to rest in each other's arms.

CHAPTER SIX

Bryan nudged her chin up with his thumb and kissed her.

"We can go up to the house and clean up if you want," he whispered in her ear.

She looked up to the hill where the big white house with blue-framed windows stood amongst trees and shook her head.

"No, I don't think so. I don't want to be an imposition."

"What are you talking about?" he frowned, not understanding what she meant.

"I know your friend said you could use the house, but that doesn't mean he'd have wanted you to bring friends in there as well. We can clean up when we get to my house, all right?" she said.

She patted his hand without even being aware of doing it. It was the kind of pat one would use to calm a disappointed child when he didn't get any ice-cream.

Bryan knew she doubted someone would let him use their house like that, but he had decided not to let her know the house belonged to him. He had chosen to play things close to the vest because he wanted her to like him for himself and not for his possessions.

He had had more than his fair share of gold-diggers and was sick of them. They wanted him for what his financial possibilities would offer them and once he refused, they had always walked away.

Bryan hoped Becka wouldn't be like that and he wanted to impress her with other things than the size of his bank account or his material possessions. He wanted her to like him for himself and he felt she did like him.

However, he was painfully aware things could change in the blink of an eye. He had met two or maybe even three women who seemed like they had been somewhat into him, but once they had found out how much money he had on his name, they fell head over heels in love with him. It hadn't lasted though. They proved afterwards they loved what he had in his pockets, and they had no interest in his mind or soul.

Becka was too important for him to let the same scenario play out, so Bryan didn't know what to do. He didn't say anything for a moment. He felt guilty because it was his fault that she felt she had to go all the way back home and clean up.

For a few seconds, he was tempted to leave it at that. His sense of self-preservation advised him not to open his big mouth and say something that might not turn too good for him. Yet, he thought better and decided to come clean, so he told her, "Becka, I have to tell you something."

His serious tone made her look up at him again. Becka didn't like where that was going. His tone made her fear the worst and after everything that had happened between them, she hoped she hadn't been wrong about him.

Becka could usually tell right away what kind of person she had before her eyes. That was one of her unique talents, even if it was raw and unrefined.

Up to that point, Bryan hadn't made her believe he was a jerk. Nothing he had done had made her doubt him.

Bryan saw the uncertainty in her eyes and it didn't sit too well with him. He wanted to alleviate her fears because he guessed what she was thinking. He still hesitated for a few moments because what he was going to tell her was against what he had decided on the yacht. Despite all that, he thought she deserved to know the truth and, besides, until then, she hadn't shown any kind of inclination towards material things.

Bryan felt a little tight squeeze in his heart thinking he could nip the relation in the bud if it turned out she was a little fortune hunter. He would suffer, in more ways than one. He had just realized he wanted her more now after he had had her than he had wanted her before. He was almost sure she was the perfect woman for him, but he was determined not to accept another relationship based only on his material status.

Bryan accepted there might not be much to him. Yet, he stubbornly clung to the thought he deserved to be with someone who wanted him, the man.

"Look, the thing is…." He started but he couldn't continue, suddenly more afraid of what she had say about his previous lie than of what he had just thought. He tried to think of the best way to explain his reasons for lying to her in the first place.

"What is it, Bryan?" Becka inquired calmly, as if the anger rising in her throat hadn't existed.

She had too much pride and didn't want to show him how much she would have cared if he had dumped her after she had fallen into his arms like a dummy, not even twenty-four hours after their initial encounter.

"You can tell me anything, it's not a problem, you know. I can take it."

"Well, there is a problem, though… I lied to you and…" he began, but he couldn't continue because she literally jumped up and stood above him like a vengeful goddess.

"Damn it, Bryan, are you married or what?" she almost screeched.

Her gaze narrowed with anger, as threatening as a snake's narrow slits, ready to kill him just with that glare.

His eyes widened and, for a few long moments, he could only stare at her. She was magnificent.

He had expected her to get upset, but he didn't expect that powerful display of anger or that she would jump to unfounded conclusions in a matter of seconds.

Becka understood he found her question way too crazy and he was rendered speechless. She slapped herself in her mind for uttering the words but she didn't know what she could say to make it right.

It took him a few more seconds to recover enough to answer to her. He stood up as well, just as angry with her accusations now, as she was with him. He looked at her incredulously with his fists on his hips.

"Of course, I'm not," he retorted with anger in his voice once he found his speech again. "I wouldn't sleep with another woman if I had been married. What the hell? What kind of a monster do you think I am?" he snapped at her, even though her hard breathing made it hard to focus.

Her generous bust was making it difficult to look anywhere else, even if he knew it was important to look only into her eyes since he didn't want to give her the wrong idea.

She calmed down then. "Well, if that's not the problem, then what is it?"

"I lied to you about that house," he said, pointing to the house on the hill with a nervous gesture.

She looked at the house and then at him, as if she hadn't understood what was going on.

"What do you mean?" she asked him after a few moments of pondering over his statement and not making any sense of it.

"That's my house, Becka. Not a friend's, but mine. I lied to you when I said a friend let me use it," he specified again, to be sure she understood him clearly.

"Oh, okay," she said, utterly appeased, and turned around to look for her bathing suit, pleased that it had nothing to do with her and that he didn't intend to let her go.

Suddenly, Becka turned back to him. Her eyes were sparking with so much fury now that he took a step back involuntarily. If he thought she looked majestic in her anger earlier, now her fury was much more than that.

Apparently, his statement had finally sunk in and she realized what he was saying. One thing was clear though: she didn't like it at all. All the implications seem a little too ugly for her to stomach them.

With a very even voice, deceitfully contradicting the wrath in her eyes, she asked him, "So why did you find it better to lie to me? Why was it so important that I didn't know the house belonged to you?"

Bryan knew her tone was deceptive and he was expecting to be hit with a full blow of her fury soon. The atmosphere was charged with electrical currents and he could feel the twinges of tension ripping in the air.

"I had a thought, you see...," he started, but stopped when he saw the mutinous stance she took.

She did look glorious in his eyes. That fury shining in her eyes, the straight back, like a poised arrow, and her small hands fisted on her hips turned her into a true piece of art.

He knew she had forgotten she didn't have a stitch of clothing on her and he appreciated her forgetfulness. His eyes betrayed his hunger while they swept over her full figure, taking in the heavy breasts and narrow waist, her lush hips and rounded thighs.

"You had a thought," she repeated, but this time her voice dripped with sarcasm.

His eyes snapped back to hers, suddenly aware he was in the middle of an argument and he shouldn't lose sight of that, if he wanted to solve the situation and leave the battlefield in one piece. She was pissed enough to take it out on him.

"Okay, I understand how that might have upset you, but you also have to understand I had my reasons..." he said, dragging the sentence away when he saw she wasn't mollified by far with his attempt to explain himself.

"Of course, you had your reasons," she snapped, throwing her hands into the air. "How could I forget that? That makes everything all right, doesn't it?"

"Becka, come on, just listen to me. It's not easy to explain what I thought," Bryan tried to reason with her.

Becka looked straight at him and said with all the sarcasm she could muster, "I'll tell you what you thought, Bryan. It's a no-brainer. You thought I was a stupid bimbo, interested in a man with money and you didn't want me to stick my greedy hands in your pockets. That's what you thought," she finished her tirade in a shout.

It sounded bad. The way she put it, it sounded very bad. Bryan felt a tinge of guilt because there was something true in her words, even though she framed his entire train of thought in an ugly manner.

"Not really, Becka. But I had my share of women who showed interest in me only because I had money and..."

Becka stomped her foot and groaned and her behavior stopped him from continuing. He waited to see what else she had to say.

She glanced at him, then she averted her eyes as if she couldn't look at him anymore. She moved to gather her swimming suit pieces and in a very quiet voice said, "I want you to take me home now."

"Please, sweetie..."

"I said now," she repeated, emphasizing her words. "I don't want to spend another moment with you. You lied to me! You thought horrible things about me!" she shouted and turned her back to him to get dressed.

He felt the pang of guilt nagging at him again, but then another thought popped into his head suddenly. Taking his pants to get dressed as well, he said sarcastically, "And you were very open with me, weren't you? You were Miss Open Book and Open Heart, weren't you?"

"What do you mean?" Becka turned back to him, stunned to hear his words. "I didn't lie to you."

"Yes, you did. You said some things yesterday and you didn't want to expand on that. Don't you remember? When you said you didn't advise me to upset you, and when you said there were things you couldn't tell me... Well, I also had things I couldn't tell you, so we are square," he concluded.

She looked at him, simmering inside. She felt her rage rise like magma inside a volcano and she couldn't hold back her anger anymore and threw her hands in the air.

A whoosh of wind swirled around him and he felt icicles on his back. The basket flew into the nearest tree trunk and the cooler followed shortly after, as if an unseen hand had lifted them and thrown them away.

Bryan felt like he was in the middle of a hurricane and watched Becka with stunned eyes. He couldn't believe what he was seeing.

Her lips started trembling and she had tears in her eyes all of a sudden. When she closed her eyes, and lowered her shaky arms, everything went back to normal. The wind stopped and the warmth of the day chased away the chills he had felt on his back.

She didn't look at him and he couldn't do anything more but stare at her in shock. He refused to think about what had happened or to find an answer, but he knew she had a hand in it and he didn't feel comfortable near her anymore.

It was sort of creepy and he couldn't find a reasonable explanation for what he had experienced and felt, and what popped into his mind didn't really make sense, but only freaked him out more.

"I think I'll take you home now," he said quietly, unwilling to go into the why's and how's right then.

Becka nodded, defeated, and started getting dressed in silence. When she finished, she went to gather the basket and the cooler. His cold voice came from behind and stopped her.

"Don't worry about those. I'll take care of everything when I come back."

Becka nodded subdued. She felt dejected and walked with small steps toward the dock. She didn't know what to tell him and she could tell he didn't want to hear anything from her right then.

She was sad because she had been having a great day with him, but that day had been built on lies and deceit and she didn't know how she felt about it anymore.

Bryan helped her on the deck of the boat with total detachment, as if she had been a woman he had just met and he had extended a customary politeness to her. Any kind of closeness they had experienced before was now gone. They felt like strangers and uncomfortable ones as that.

Once on the boat, she went under the canopy and put on her t-shirt and pants, while he went to the helm and started the boat, speeding up as soon as it was possible.

Bryan didn't feel like being with her anymore, at least for the moment, but he imagined his feelings would go back to normal once he had time to think about things. The man felt some guilt over his omissions, but he considered she was much more at fault for the situation than him.

He didn't want to dwell on what had happened because he didn't like what he read into the facts. Despite all that, he also felt regret because he felt something for her, even though their relationship had developed only in the span of a day. He had thought she was the one for him and it was hard to think it was just an illusion. He needed time to think about all of that.

Becka was upset with him and with herself at the same time. She was upset he had felt the need to keep his wealth a secret, fearing she would be more attracted to that than to him. She would have liked for him to trust her and to think differently about her.

She could understand past experiences might have made him fearful about people's reasons. However, she thought she had been open enough and she normally didn't make people think she was a person who would take advantage of a man. She didn't seem a woman with greedy little hands ready to grasp everything in sight.

Becka was also mad at herself because she had no control over her powers. Whenever she would get mad, she would unleash them and she couldn't stop anything.

Becka knew people didn't take it lightly when someone made things float in the air and brought icy swirls of wind around them. Her mother had told her that over and over again since she was a baby and she was famous for throwing serious tantrums. Luckily, she had learned her lesson before going out into the real world.

Unfortunately, she had forgotten all those lessons today. She hadn't walked away from the fight with Bryan, and she had put herself on the spot. She had chased Bryan away because he had to be too freaked out now to want to stay with her.

She didn't like how cold and detached he behaved then. After that wonderful afternoon, when they shared those precious moments together, for which she had been waiting for a long time, his demeanour had the effect of a cold shower. His present cold attitude tainted everything.

Becka wasn't sorry she had made love to Bryan. She would have lied to herself if she had said that. However, she was sorry because the aftermath had turned out so bleak and left her feeling so empty.

Becka didn't realize she was crying already, but Bryan heard her sobs and turned to her. A claw squeezed his heart.

For a fleeting moment, he thought he would better mind his business and let her cry. He wasn't very good around a crying woman. He should let her sort things out first and then try to approach her, but he couldn't let go.

That woman had already had a huge impact on him and regardless what he was feeling that very moment, he couldn't stand idle by and let her cry without offering her any kind of solace.

When she felt his hand on her shoulder, Becka looked up. Bryan saw the tears running down her cheeks. He dried them with his thumb and pulled her up and into his arms, rubbing her back. He rested his head on hers and just held her, softly stroking her back to calm her down and make her feel better.

"It's all right, baby, you don't have to cry. It's not the end of the world, you know," he murmured.

His words made her cry harder and through hiccups she said, "It's the end of us, Bryan, and that's the end of the world now."

He smiled, slightly amused and raised her head to look into her eyes and kissed her lips softly, longing to feel her close to him again.

"I don't know if it's the end of us, but both of us have some thinking to do, Becka, and then we'll see," he said evenly.

"You want me to explain?" she asked with hesitation in her voice.

He shook his head, "No, not right now. I must think for a while and then we can talk. It's better not to talk about anything right now."

"Why does it have to be on your timetable?" she snapped at him, forgetting about her sadness for a moment.

"It's not on my timetable," he tried to be reasonable. "It's something I have to do, though. I do have to think. You can't think I'll just put everything behind and go on without any questions, sweetie, because, believe me, it doesn't work that way," he said in an even tone, although he felt like strangling her for being so dense.

It wasn't like everything that had happened was everyday stuff. He had already come up with an explanation, but he didn't like it, even though that possibility was nudging more and more at him. More importantly, he didn't know if his feelings were strong enough for him to continue being in a relationship with a woman who could create a small storm. He liked to have a certain balance in everything and his relationship with Becka wasn't balanced by far.

Becka pulled away and turned her back to him. She understood her show might have freaked him out, but she didn't understand why he didn't want to talk about it.

She had been told never to show her heritage to strangers, but she thought she would have a chance at a real relationship with him and she had to show him what she could do. It happened earlier than she had hoped, but she didn't think it was such a bad thing, quite the opposite.

She tried to console herself with the thought that, at least, she didn't invest too much in a relationship with no chance of survival.

"Becka…" Bryan started to say but she put her hand up to make him stop.

She didn't turn back to him when she said, "Everything is fine, Bryan, don't worry. I understand your reluctance. Let's just go home and forget we've ever met."

Her voice showed more determination than she felt but she didn't want him to stick around only because he felt sorry that she cried. If he couldn't be with her for what she was, then she didn't see a point in continuing with the charade.

"It might not be so simple, Becka. I didn't say we should forget we've met. I just asked for a little time to process what happened. Maybe that time would work for you, too."

"Whatever you say," she shrugged and went to the other side of the boat to get away from him.

In a way, Becka knew Bryan was right. It wasn't as if he had had to get over a bad habit like talking with her mouth full. Yet, she felt cheated because she had jumped into an affair with him without thinking it over.

She didn't like he had lied to her, either. Everything was too much for her to forgive right then. She didn't even think it was worth the trouble.

The rest of the trip was made in total silence. They stole glances at each other, but neither one of them wanted to talk anymore.

When they got to the harbor, they moored the yacht and went to the parking lot where he had left the car in the morning.

The tension grew more during the car ride. The car was too small to contain both their resentments and heartaches. They started to dislike each other immensely and couldn't wait to get to their destination and part ways.

Bryan had hardly stopped the car when Becka jumped out, throwing a quick good-bye over her shoulder and ran to her house. As soon as she was inside, she shut the door behind her with a resonant bang.

Bryan looked after her and even five minutes later he was still there, in front of her house, staring at the closed door. That bang had sounded like a bad omen to him.

Bryan didn't feel as relieved as he had previously thought. While on the boat, on their way back to town, he had wanted just to drive Becka home and be done with everything for that day. Now, though, it felt like Becka had slammed the door over the only good thing that had happened in his life.

The man thought about going to her door and demanding she talked to him, but he nipped the thought in the bud. It wasn't the right moment. Even he, with his limited social skills when it came to love relationships, knew that.

Bryan needed to give her room to cool off and he needed time to mull things over and find a better way to deal with what had happened. That decision made him turn his key in the ignition and drive his car away.

CHAPTER SEVEN

Becka was in the garden, staring into the distance. For a few days now, she couldn't find any peace there, although it used to be her realm of tranquility before.

She hadn't even gone to classes anymore and she couldn't seem able to do anything. She couldn't even read one of the books she loved to read or chat with her cousins. She would chat with one of them at least once a day and now it had already been a week and a half and she still couldn't pick up the phone and call any of them.

Becka had avoided seeing anyone over the past week and a half since her falling out with Bryan. She hadn't felt able to go to the regular dinner with her parents. She had made up a party she couldn't miss, only to get out of it.

Her father hadn't been too happy about it, but her mother had exulted hearing that her daughter finally had a social life befitting a young girl of her age. She'd always thought Becka was too introverted when it came to making friends and she didn't like it.

It was Friday again and, this time, she knew that next day she wouldn't be able to avoid dinner with her parents anymore. Her great-grandmother would be there and not even her mother would find the words to apologize for Becka's absence. When great-grandmother came to dinner, everyone had to attend. Only being bedridden in the hospital would have been a valid excuse.

Becka didn't know what she should do. She was sure everyone would immediately see that something had happened to her and she was heartbroken.

She'd seen her face in the mirror when she brushed her teeth day after day. She knew she looked exactly like she felt, as if her very life had been crushed out of her.

Becka couldn't get over what had happened with Bryan. She had fallen for him hard and no matter how much she rationalized what she felt, she couldn't make those feelings go away.

She knew it was just less than two full weeks, but she was afraid she would always think about him and it would be difficult for her to find another man who would complete her so well.

Now, with a cool mind, she realized her outburst about the house shouldn't have happened. They had known each other for a day only and he had the right to protect himself if he had been burnt before. Hadn't she reacted to that lie so strongly, everything would have been fine and she could have revealed the truth about herself to him later when he could have accepted who she was.

Unfortunately, it was too late to think of that now. She had managed to find a great guy and lose it in two dates. Probably that was a record.

***

Bryan rang the bell and waited for Becka to open the door. He had taken residence in hell since their break up over some stupid words and a little magic.

He had chosen to think of what she had done in terms of *a little magic* because it just seemed easier to understand and accept. Bryan knew they would have to talk about that too, but he had already decided to keep an open mind and not just give up because of what she was.

Initially, the man had tried hard to forget her. Owning a dojo helped him spend the days in excruciating effort. He tried exercising and lifting weights. Then he progressed to boxing. He made a point in having a date with the boxing bag every day for hours, but that didn't work.

After the first few days, he left his friend in charge and he progressed to drinking. After the first hangover, he remembered why he had hated drinking. He had always disliked not being in total control and drinking had that power over him. After the first bottle of scotch, his reactions would slow down and he would hate himself.

In the end, he had just wasted hours after hours thinking of Becka and what he should have done differently or how he should have reacted to get a different result.

Even though their relationship had had such a short span of life, it marked him deeply. He would hear her voice all the time and he would dream of her when he finally could fall asleep.

After a week and a half, Bryan decided he had had enough. He had to go over to her and try to fix everything so he could bring her back into his life. He knew he couldn't go on like that. She had become too important to him and he couldn't just forget her.

Bryan was sure she had something to do with magic, but in the great scheme of things, that didn't matter to him anymore. He was willing to put up with that if she would find it in her heart to take him back.

That was why now, he was waiting patiently for her to come and open the door.

The echo of the bell had already faded away and she still hadn't come to the door. Bryan was stubborn enough though and, with determination, rang the bell again. He resigned himself to wait with his hands in his pocket, rocking on the balls of his feet.

When a few minutes passed and still there was no sign of Becka, Bryan shrugged and instinctively tried the knob of the door. Of course, as expected, the door wasn't locked. He swore under his breath, thinking of the worst, and entered the house, closing the door quietly behind him.

Bryan felt like an interloper for a moment and thought of the consequences of his venture. Yet, he was determined to see his quest had a happy ending so he called her name.

The silence of the house weighed down on him. He didn't hear steps coming down the stairs and decided to go into the kitchen. The room was empty, but then again, he could see Becka through the window, sitting under the gazebo, at the other end of the garden.

The woman looked small and lost, with her hands folded in her lap. There was a faraway look on her face that tugged at his heart. Happy because he had found her, Bryan went out in the garden and walked towards her.

Becka didn't seem to notice she wasn't alone anymore. When he got closer to her, he saw the signs showing she had cried and he felt like a jerk.

She seemed tired and defeated and his heart ached a little more knowing he was the one who put that expression on her face.

"Becka," he called her name softly when he stepped under the canopy.

She sighed, but didn't say anything and didn't glance at him. That wasn't a good sign. Bryan panicked at the thought she had decided to ignore him, shut him out of her life and not to talk to him anymore.

"Becka," he called her more forcefully and only then, she turned to him with a soft gasp.

Her eyes grew wide and he could see she couldn't believe he was there.

"I rang the bell twice," he said to explain his presence in her garden. "I tried the door only because I saw you didn't answer and I thought you didn't lock it."

"I can't hear the bell from here," she said quietly. "It wasn't intentional," she continued. "I mean it wasn't like I didn't want to open the door for you."

He shook his head to chase her worries away and said, "I didn't think about that, sweetie. I just told you why I came inside so you wouldn't think I'm some damn stalker."

Becka gave him a small smile, but her face didn't glow as it used to do before and that didn't sit right with him.

"But why are you here, Bryan? Nothing changed from the last week as far as I know. You still think I'm a gold digger, I know you're a liar and we both know what I can do."

Bryan didn't like her resigned tone, nor did he like the sadness he read on her face. He didn't like her accusation either. He knelt before her and took one of her hands in both of his, and stroked them gently.

"I don't think you're a gold digger, baby, and I never thought that. Maybe it was stupid of me to wait and see if you liked me for me at first, but I really had some bad experiences in the past and I guess… I just needed some reassurance. I hope you can forgive my stupidity."

"And what about what happened when we argued?" she asked with hesitation. She was afraid to hear his answer.

Bryan stood up and sat on the bench, pulling her into his lap.

"Well… That was something else, Becka, I must say… Nothing I've experienced before, I am sure. Maybe you can explain it to me because… It freaked me out, Becka," he admitted in a grave voice. "I've never seen something like that and, of course, the first thing I thought was that you are… a…" Bryan started to say but he couldn't continue and say exactly what he thought.

"A witch?" she asked matter-of-factly.

Bryan didn't answer immediately. He pondered on what he remembered first.

"I don't know… I thought of a poltergeist or something like that," he confessed in the end, staring at her.

"Oh, gosh, I haven't thought you'd think that," she exclaimed. "I'm not anything like that, Bryan, be serious."

Bryan narrowed his eyes and asked, "So what are you exactly? Not that it would matter, to be honest," he rushed to add.

"What do you mean it wouldn't matter?"

He took a few moments to consider his answer. He looked over the garden, absently stroking her hip.

"All right, I'll be honest with you," he said looking back at her. "I can't function. I can't sleep and I can't do anything, as a matter of fact. I've tried and nothing works. I'm thinking only of you. So, no matter what, I want to be with you. So you know."

Seeing her eyes trained straight on him, he amended his statement, "If you want the same thing too, of course. I can't force you, I know that. But I hope you do want me too."

Becka stroked the side of his face with tenderness and leaned to kiss him on the lips.

"I want to, but I think you do need to know everything before going any further," she said with sadness.

"Just tell me," Bryan said. "I'm sure it's not so dramatic and anyway, I think I can live with what you are. Considering I can't live without having you in my life, the point is moot, as you say. I know it sounds pretentious, but then again you should know the days we've been apart were a living hell for me."

"All right, Bryan. I'll tell you then," Becka started and then stopped.

She couldn't make the words come out as, too afraid he would run away again.

"Come on, baby, just say it. I promise everything will be fine."

"Huh!" she scoffed.

Her distrust was evident and he knew he deserved that. He had already run away from her once. He chose to look at her with insistence and make her talk. She held his stare and finally went on with her explanation.

"So, how can I tell you this, Bryan? I think I should be direct," she murmured and he made efforts to hear her. "All right, here it is," she started again. "I'm a witch and unfortunately not a very good one. I still have to learn to control the gift. You saw what happens if I get angry," she told him and he nodded. "In general, I try to walk out of confrontations because of that, but with you, then, I didn't have the space to do it. You see, when I get mad, all those intense feelings turn into icy gushes of wind and things start flying around and that's something I can't stop. I don't have the knowledge to do it," she explained to make him understand.

"All right, fair enough," he said. "What else can you do?" he asked in a conversational tone, although he didn't feel very at ease hearing his worst fears voiced out, and knowing he didn't have a choice in the matter.

"Not much. That thing and... I can tell if people are all right or not. I can't tell if they're felons or killers or anything like that. I can tell though if they give me a good vibe or not," she shrugged.

"And I gave you a good vibe, I understand," Bryan assumed and she nodded. "So, let's sum it up, Becka. You're a witch and I'm wealthy. Is there anything else that should be said?"

She shrugged again and shook her head. They stayed silent for a while, when she decided to ask, "Should I tell you everyone in my family is a witch?"

He looked at her surprised and said, "Really? Everybody? And all of them do the same things as you?"

She laughed, seeing he looked so bewildered, and answered.

"No, not everyone can do the same thing. Some can read minds, some can heal. Everyone has their gift. Of course, we all can do basic stuff, but some of us chose not to do it anymore. I don't. It's not like I can get very far right now, so..."

"Why?" he asked completely surprised to hear all she had to say.

"This is the part I can't tell you... Or at least not now... Not if there is a chance to be together... And if we are meant to be together, you'll find out when the time is right. I hope you'll understand and don't pressure me to…"

Bryan stopped her with a finger on her lips.

"You don't have to tell me anything now if you can't. We passed over the first hurdle, let's keep it that way. When you're ready and you can, you'll tell me, okay?"

Becka looked at him with hope, but she didn't dare to hope too much. Her heart still ached and she didn't know if she could take another rejection from him. The first time had been enough.

"Will we be together, Bryan?"

Bryan gathered her to him and hugged her. She felt he didn't want to let her go anymore.

"Yes, if you want to be with me and you can forgive me for the way I reacted that day at the lake, yes, we can be together, sweetheart."

She nodded and, smiling, hugged him back as hard as she could. She cuddled as close as possible to him and sighed with content.

Bryan was happy to see her so willing to get over the argument they had had and get back together. He was satisfied to sit there with her wrapped in his arms and just listen to the silence of the garden.

The light changed and the evening came with a pale wind, which hushed through the multitude of flowers populating Becka's garden. They were still cuddled together and none of them felt like letting go.

Becka's head rested on Bryan's chest and Bryan held her tight. He rested his chin on the top of her head and enjoyed the unusual scent of her hair.

"Do you want to come inside with me?" Becka whispered after a while. "Maybe spend the night with me?"

Bryan smiled and lifted her head to see if she blushed. He wasn't disappointed. A faint blush had already colored her cheeks and her eyes were twinkling in the twilight.

He couldn't resist and took her mouth in a kiss that held all that desire he had felt for her during the days he couldn't see her.

Still kissing her, he stood up with her snuggled up in his arms and started towards the house. Only when they got to the kitchen door, he raised his head and looked at her again, then, balancing her on one knee, he opened the door and took her inside, closing the door with his foot behind them.

"So, where's your bedroom?" he asked her, crossing through the kitchen.

"Upstairs, the last room on the left," she answered breathless, unable to believe he would carry her all the way upstairs. It was so romantic that her little heart sang.

He kissed her again for good measure and carried her to the bedroom. Once inside her bedroom, he let her stand and looked for the switch to turn the light on but she beat him to it. The strong light burnt his eyes and he blinked a few times.

Once his eyes got used to the light, Bryan swept the room with his eyes and had to grin.

That room spoke loud and clear about Becka. It was a room with the air of the turn of the century, cluttered with pillows and comfortable armchairs on one side. On the other side of the room, a big, antique chest of drawers took most of the wall and was covered with photos showing groups of people, some young and some old, and knick-knacks, all of them fairies, etheric and whimsical. Behind the armchairs, a wide window showed the garden he still could see although it was already dark outside. The window had a large bench built in, covered in thick colorful pillows and he could imagine Becka lying there, reading.

He turned back to Becka and saw she was observing him carefully, as if she had wanted to guess what he was thinking.

"I like your bedroom, Becka. It's got you written all over it. Too many pillows for my taste, but, what the heck, it works for you."

She smiled brightly and advanced towards him with her lazy stride. Her summer dress covered her legs only up to her knees and he enjoyed the sight of her shapely legs in her slow journey towards him. The two straps, holding the dress on her shoulders, didn't cover much and he found her more enticing than if she'd been modelling a sexy nighty.

When she reached him, Becka leaned in and kissed him softly on the lips. That fleeting kiss made him burn even more for her.

He pulled her into his arms and kissed her soundly, molding her lips to his, nibbling at her lower lip, all the while stroking her shoulders and arms and her back.

He gazed into her eyes again to see if she really wanted to make love to him. He needed to be sure because he couldn't go through another fight and another break-up.

When he saw she was on the same page with him, he unzipped her dress and lowered the straps of the dress to reveal her generous bust. He licked his lips in his hunger to feel her nipple in his mouth and lowered his head to satisfy his craving. She sighed and moaned and tried to keep her balance while he started the sweet torture she enjoyed so much.

He led her back to the bed and helped her lie down, then showed her how much he needed to make love to her.

CHAPTER EIGHT

Bryan got out of the shower, whistling. He was in a very good mood that day. He had had a beautiful night with Becka and he had enjoyed her lack of shyness in bed, even though she was timid out of bed.

The young woman was something else, indeed. She had proved she was everything he needed during the long night they had spent together, but also during the first part of his shower, ended with a shared passion.

Bryan realized he was happy. That was a feeling he hadn't had in such a long time, he couldn't even remember when he had been happy before, if he had ever been.

It wasn't just their lovemaking, although it was an interesting experience to make love to Becka. She was open to learn how to make love to him and how to enjoy the pleasures with which he showered her.

Besides that, there was also the pleasure of talking to her. She was not a woman to prattle away about fashion or other things men didn't understand. She could touch an eclectic group of subjects and kept surprising him with her insight.

Bryan had told her a few things from his past. Of course, he kept silent about the worst ones, because he didn't want to scare her away. He hoped he would be able to share those with her in time. However, he had told her about some of the things he had done, because he wanted her to know that nothing about him was just in white and black.

Bryan thought she needed to know the man she got involved with, because, ultimately, all his experiences had had a hand in making him the man he had become and she loved. He told her about his dojo and she showed interest in seeing it and she even wanted to train with him, so he told her that he would take her there the following week.

She had also revealed her dreams and she had told him stories about her childhood and teen years. He had heard a few things about her cousins and siblings, and it made him understand that Becka's family was a close-knit one.

They were close to each other, not like his own. He had admitted he hadn't seen his father in over twenty-five years, since he took off. The old man couldn't live with his mother anymore. Her sharp tongue had weakened his will to keep his marriage together and strengthened his wish to live as far as possible from her. Once he left, he didn't look back anymore, not even to check on his son.

His mother was another story altogether. She was still present in his life, if only to make his life a living hell whenever they would get together. She considered it was his duty as a son to visit her at least once a month and she took great pleasure in cutting him to size, as she used to say, during those monthly visits.

Now Becka knew he didn't love his mother anymore. He had probably stopped loving her when he was five. She was verbally abusing everyone with an odd pleasure and she considered everybody was beneath her station. Her son had been good for various things along the years, but he hadn't been good enough to love.

Yet, he had taken care of her. She had her own house and a monthly alimony for a comfortable living so he didn't feel guilty at all for not looking after her, even though she tried to make him feel that way every chance she got.

Bryan dried himself with a towel and got dressed in a rush. He knew Becka was in the kitchen. She had promised him to cook breakfast for him and he was a little concerned. He had proposed to cook breakfast for both of them, but she insisted. She said it was the only meal of the day she could cook, so she wanted to show off her culinary talents.

Bryan smiled remembering the way she had sounded. He had promised himself to praise her efforts even if her cooking lacked any skill.

He went downstairs still whistling and headed directly to the kitchen. His sweet Becka was swearing loud. He heard her all the way from the hallway and grinned. He hadn't thought she would know some of those words.

Something had happened with the eggs apparently. Becka had wanted to make sunny-side up eggs, but the eggs had refused to cooperate with her.

The grin on his lips grew wider. Bryan didn't care if he ate scrambled eggs or sunny-side up eggs or whatever. He cared she had gone through all that trouble to make breakfast for him. He couldn't remember any woman who had made him breakfast.

Bryan entered the kitchen and for a second there, the man couldn't hide his shock. The sight overwhelmed him. Luckily, Becka was facing the stove and mumbling so she didn't hear him coming in.

The kitchen was in shambles. With a hand on his heart, he vowed never to let her in the kitchen again even if that meant he would have to cook well into his old age.

The woman had made a complete and total chaos. And that under fifteen minutes. The pristine kitchen from the night before looked now as if a hurricane had passed through it and turned everything upside down.

Now, he knew why her kitchen had looked untouched the night before. Probably she didn't cook at all.

"May I help you, Becka?" he asked and Becka shrieked and dropped on the floor the spatula she had in her hand. She had been so focused on what she was doing that he had scared the hell out of her.

"I'm sorry, baby," he rushed to her. "I thought you heard me coming. I was whistling so...," he said, reaching down and taking the spatula from the floor and throwing it into the sink.

"Not a problem, Bryan. You just gave me a heart attack," she said with all the dramatic flair she could muster, pressing her little hand over her heart. "I was just finishing up breakfast. Coffee is already on the table. Go and pour yourself a cup and I'll bring the rest, okay?"

He nodded, but the moment she turned back to the stove, he shook his head. He couldn't believe one person could do so much damage while cooking breakfast. It was unimaginable.

In her hurry to do everything, she had thrown the eggshells on the counter, next to the bacon package and carton of eggs, also forgotten there. There were breadcrumbs everywhere.

Something was burning and he guessed it was the toast. He was right. The fire alarm set off and he rushed to open the kitchen door to the garden so the smoke would dissipate sooner.

Then he went to the toaster in a hurry and took the bread out.

By then, Becka had started crying. She had tried her best and her best failed her. She had known she didn't have any cooking skills, but she had thought she could make breakfast, once in her life, without having everything go wrong and, more important, without setting off the fire alarm.

Breakfast was the only meal she was brave enough to try. Becka was afraid if she tried something more elaborate, her kitchen would go up in flames.

However, today she had wanted to impress Bryan. Well, she impressed him, all right. That was sure. But then, it was not the impression she had wanted to give him.

Becka was crying in earnest now, and as much as he wanted to, Bryan couldn't go to comfort her. There was no time for that. He had more pressing matters to take care of.

After turning off the toaster and taking the toast out, Bryan rushed to the stove where the eggs were slowly turning into a black-reddish mass. He was sure the fire alarm would soon rouse all the neighbors.

With efficient and measured gestures, he took the pan off the stove and threw it in the sink. A look at those eggs told him he couldn't save them anymore. Shaking his head, he returned to the stove and turned it off as well.

Bryan looked around and picked the eggshells abandoned on the counter and threw them in the garbage. The man wiped his hands with a kitchen towel and returned the bacon back in the fridge.

After a last survey of the kitchen, Bryan washed his hands and then, finally went to Becka and slid an arm behind her. He gathered to his chest and kissed the corner of her mouth tenderly. He nudged her head up and brushed her tears away with his thumb.

"It's all right baby, it's not the end of the world, all right? Come on, stop crying now and let's eat the bacon and toast. I think they're okay. We'll have some coffee and everything will be fine. If you're still hungry after we finish breakfast, we can go to Timmie's and have something to eat there, all right?"

"I wanted everything to be perfect," she wailed, making him smile and kiss her once more.

"Everything's perfect, honey," he reassured her and hugged her again.

"How can you say that?" she shouted. "The eggs were a failure from the beginning and that stupid fire alarm won't stop…"

"It's stopped now. Look, no shrilling sounds. The room is aired, see? The smoke is gone. Look, it's stopped," he comforted her again after the last beep of the alarm finally died out.

"I wanted to make something nice for you," she sobbed.

Becka didn't understand why she was so emotional and why she couldn't stop sobbing. Come to think of it, she had never cried like that before the last few days and she had never been a mass of tangled emotions.

"Come on, stop crying, Becka," he shook her gently. "You did. You did something nice for me. No one has ever bothered to make me a cup of coffee at least so you've done more than anyone else in my life. Please, now, stop crying. It's all right," he patted her back to reassure her.

Becka hiccupped a couple of times and allowed him to lead her to the table and help her sit down. Bryan poured coffee and they started munching on the toast, which was thoroughly black, and on the bacon, which, happily, was only partially burnt.

Both tried to ignore the crunching sounds filling the kitchen. It was as if a battalion of mice was munching at the same time.

"I do appreciate your effort, sweetie, but from now on, I'll cook, okay?" Bryan told her in between two bites. "And I do want you to promise me you won't ever try to cook again. You want a homemade meal, I'm available. Anytime, day or night, I'm here for you. Just don't try to cook again. I wouldn't want to hear your kitchen went up in flames," he urged her, his mind filled with horrible scenarios.

Becka nodded, keeping her eyes down, but she didn't say a thing. She felt her failure deeply and she couldn't look him in the eyes.

She had never cared about her inability to cook before, but now her inaptitude in the kitchen felt like a failure and she was sorry she didn't take her Aunt Marjorie up on her offer to teach her how to cook.

Bryan nudged her head up and smiled at her. He leaned over to kiss her and then said, "You're a real treasure, baby, believe me. You don't have to feel ashamed. I'm sure you can do things I can't, so everything levels just fine."

She nodded again, but didn't reply. They continued to eat their breakfast in silence.

"Any plans for today?" he asked her.

"I haven't made any plans for days," she confessed shaking her head. "I didn't feel like it."

"I'm sorry I upset you so much," he apologized, but she waved his concern away.

"It was my fault as well, so… Anyway, tonight I'm forced to go to a family dinner. Would you like to come with me?"

Bryan suddenly felt a constriction in his throat. Going to a family dinner was a big thing. He couldn't say it was too soon because he already knew how he felt about her, even though they had known each other for so little time. The week and a half without Becka wasn't something he would like to remember or relive. Yet, meeting her family hadn't crossed his mind.

Bryan looked at Becka and saw the hope in her eyes. He felt like an ogre for wanting to say 'no'. So, he agreed to go with her.

Hearing his answer, Becka jumped off her chair and directly onto his lap, peppering his face with kisses, and making him laugh. He was content she was so happy with his decision.

CHAPTER NINE

Bryan was sitting in his idle car in front of Becka's house. He'd been sitting there for almost fifteen minutes already, and still couldn't find his courage to get out and ring her doorbell to let her know he was there.

He was wearing his dress pants and a white shirt, although he wasn't very sure it was the right attire to meet her entire family. He had thought of wearing his best dress suit at first, but the evening was too hot and he didn't think he could wear a coat. Besides, he absolutely hated wearing a tie. It always felt as if someone had strangled him and he already felt his throat was a little too tight. He didn't want to add more to his discomfort.

That evening was a first for him. In none of his previous relationships, had he made it so far. Bryan had never met the parents of the women he had dated. Maybe because he hadn't been so much into the woman he was dating or maybe because it hadn't ever felt like the right moment. There had always been reasons and he had always declined to show up at such gatherings. This time, he knew he couldn't back out of that dinner.

The man wanted Becka in his life. He was positive about that. He knew having a real relationship with her meant that he, unfortunately, had to meet the pesky parents, as well.

Family was a pivotal pylon in Becka's life from what he had gathered from her, and he couldn't treat that with indifference.

Beside the thought of getting together with her family, which would have worried any man meeting the parents for the first time, he also worried he would have to go directly into a den of witches.

Witches had never crossed his mind before he witnessed what Becka could do. He had always written such things off as just a hoax.

That day, at the lake, he had been forced to reconsider his beliefs. Nothing else would have explained what had happened.

Had it not been for the icy swirls of wind gushing around him, he would have gone with telekinesis, which seemed to border on being a somewhat more scientific fact. He would have possibly thought of hypnosis, which also appeared a more valid theory, but then, considering the circumstances, that didn't make the cut. They were in the middle of a fight so Becka couldn't have hypnotize him no matter how good she might have been.

When nothing else worked, he had to go with what might have seemed unreasonable, yet the only possibility.

Becka had told him a little about each of her family members so he wouldn't feel he was plunging into the unknown with no information at all. Yet, that didn't assuage his worries.

The idea that someone could read his mind or could turn the entire meal into a bunch of frogs had the power to render him a little more skeptical about his wisdom to make that visit. A sane man wouldn't go into something like that if he hadn't been hit over the head with something first, and then dragged into the lair.

But then, he couldn't have refused her invitation if he had wanted to continue seeing Becka and have her in his life and he did.

Bryan glanced at the dashboard clock and saw it was almost time to go and ring the bell. He had arrived earlier because he knew he would need some more time to reconsider everything and make up his mind or, more precisely, to pretend doing that. His decision had already been made the day before when he came to convince Becka to give him a new chance.

With a deep sigh, he got out of his car and with resolute but resigned steps, not unlike the ones of the people on their way to guillotine, he went to Becka's door and rang the doorbell.

Bryan was positive her door would be unlocked given what he knew about her, but he didn't want to make her believe he considered he could come and go from her house at will.

The theme of *Jaws* made him smile again and he felt more at ease with his choice than he was a few moments ago. Her hurried steps sounded on the wooden floor of the hall and he imagined her running to open the door for him. That image in his head made his heart grow a little.

He wasn't wrong. At the sound of the bell, Becka had rushed down the stairs, leaving her hair down. She had tried to make up her mind about how to fix her hair for the last fifteen minutes. She knew it didn't matter how her hair would look in the eyes of her family, but she wanted to look perfect for Bryan.

Becka had thought her feelings for him were strong before he came back to her the day before, but then, after spending that night and half a day with him, her feelings had grown much stronger.

She was determined to make their relationship work because without him she had been miserable and life had been bleak. She didn't want to go through all that again.

Becka opened the door, a little out of breath, and beamed at him. Bryan pulled her into his arms and kissed her soundly as if he hadn't seen her for days, even though only a few hours had passed since they said good-bye.

She wrapped her arms around his neck and let herself feel his passion. His kiss made her forget about the dinner with her family and anything else she might have had on her mind. She didn't even care that someone could see them from the street. It only mattered that she was in his arms and he seemed to love and desire her enough.

Bryan couldn't let go of her. It took him a few long kisses before he was able to pull back. Only then, he returned her smile. Every fiber in his body was alert, screaming for her.

He didn't understand how he had fallen so hard for that woman in such a short period of time, but he was in love, head over heels, a feeling he had never experienced before. Suddenly, a strange thought crossed his mind and he frowned.

"What's the matter?" Becka asked, seeing his frown, and concern shadowed her face.

Bryan watched her steadily, thinking how to frame his question, and only after a few seconds of pondering over the matter, he found his courage to ask her about what puzzled him.

"Don't take it wrong, Becka, okay, but I need to know something… Is what I feel for you the result of a spell or… the real thing?"

Becka scowled at him and pulled back with a gasp. Then she launched herself furiously forward and punched his chest as hard as she could with her fist.

"How can you ask me something like that? You… you… you're a jerk."

She punched him again for good measure and tried to slam the door in his face but his arm blocked her move.

"Becka, be reasonable, baby."

"I'll show you reasonable, you… you… you… ass!" she yelled and, turning her back to him, she stormed out of the hallway into the living room like a little fury.

Behind her, the hallway wardrobe opened with a resounding thump and all the coats hanging inside flew out and swirled to the floor in a rain of colors.

Bryan only shook his head with resignation and followed her inside, stepping carelessly over the clothes lining the floor of the hallway.

This time, he was prepared for her storms and didn't mind walking into the lion's den. He imagined he would be safe enough because she liked him sufficiently. He thought she wouldn't truly try to hurt him.

He did hope he wasn't wrong since he didn't know what a witch could, in fact, do. The thought that he should have researched the subject a little, to be more informed and prepared, crossed his mind, but it was too late to do anything about that.

He found her at the window in the living room with tears in her eyes and his heart ached to see her so desolate. He hated himself because he was the reason for her tears, yet again.

The day before, he had promised himself he would do his best not to make her cry anymore and not even a day later, he did it again.

"Sweetheart," he called out to her in a soft voice. "Come on, don't cry," he said putting a hand on her shoulder.

He tried to soothe her, although he didn't have too much experience with soothing. He would just go away whenever a woman started crying. This time, he couldn't walk away.

Becka shook his hand off her shoulder and rubbed her fingers over her face to dry the tears away. Then, she turned to him and looked at him sadly, but with determination.

After watching him for a few moments, she said, "You'd better go, Bryan. If this is what you think about me, then it's clear there's no chance for us to be together, so we shouldn't waste our time anymore."

Bryan felt an icy wall rising between them and for the first time in his life he felt scared. His mind raced to find a way to persuade her they still had a chance, but after struggling for a few moments, he concluded he would better go with the truth.

"All right, sweetie, here's the deal."

At his words, Becka looked up at him, but kept quiet, allowing him to continue. She seriously considered to deck him if he had said anything hurtful again. At least, she could try.

"I want you too much, baby, and I'm pretty sure my liking you so much means that I love you. It's a too strong feeling to be something else. Now, considering I've never been in love in my entire life, and I do mean never," he emphasized his words, "and this is happening so fast, I had to ask myself if it might have been something you did. It's not like me," he pleaded.

She was narrowing her eyes in anger and that foretold a new storm, so he rushed with his explanation.

"That being said, it doesn't mean I have any kind of bad thoughts about you. Far from that! I just wanted to make sure it was me who loved you. Without any external interference. You understand?"

Becka didn't reply. She just kept looking at him, weighing his words. She could see why he would interpret things like that. A man at his age who had never been in love would have been bound to question the validity of his feelings, especially if everything had happened too fast. That was understandable. It hurt though that, even for a moment, he thought his feelings were induced by a spell.

She nodded to show him she could see the validity of his argument, and then said, "I understand what you mean. It's a valid reasoning, that's true. That doesn't mean it doesn't hurt, Bryan, because it hurts like hell... Listen to me, Bryan. Being a witch doesn't automatically mean you can do whatever you want. There are limitations and boundaries. You can't step over boundaries because there are consequences. And, besides that, who the hell would want to make someone fall in love with them and live with the knowledge that their love is not real? Tell me!" she asked him and slapped his chest.

He pulled her into his arms, kissing the top of her head and whispered to her, "I didn't mean to hurt you. I just wanted to be sure it was me."

"All right, then. What now? Do you want to break up with me or what? Because I don't know if there's a way to prove it to you. I can yell it from the top of the roofs but that doesn't prove anything."

He pushed her at arm's length and looked at her with disbelief.

"Are you serious? How would breaking up with you make it better? There's no doubt I want to be with you. Where do you find these ideas?"

Becka shrugged again and he thought he did find that habit of hers charming. She looked like a naughty schoolgirl and for a moment, the thought she was way too young for him popped into his mind and he struggled to fight it back.

Bryan didn't want to think of anything that might have worked against their relationship, but then, in a way, he felt like a thief, who was stealing her youth. He considered to tell her that, but decided against it. She enjoyed drama and quite a lot and he didn't want to use up all his resources to calm her again. He was sure he would need those while he visited with her family.

It wasn't that he didn't appreciate her dramas. Becka had flair for a good scene and she looked very authentic. It was ingrained in her.

Now, that he was thinking of that, he realized she was the first woman whose drama he had ever enjoyed. He used to walk out of the door whenever a woman tried her theatricals with him. If that wasn't a sign he was in deep, he didn't know what else to look for.

Bryan looked at her from the top of her head to her toes. He loved how the white dress hugged her curves. It stopped a palm over the knees, which left the better part of her beautiful legs in sight.

He appreciated the fact she would wear white. Most women would try to wear only black or other dark colors merely to entertain the illusion that they looked thinner. The man admired Becka because her originality was refreshing. He liked she felt well in her own skin and she was able to see herself as beautiful as he saw her.

"By the way, you look great, baby. Your family will be stunned to see you with me. I should have worn a tie or something. Your dress is elegant and I look like a slob. As if I'd had no knowledge about fashion or choosing clothes," he shook his head in regret.

"Be serious, Bryan," she waved his concerns away. "You look just fine. It suits you and I want you, not the replica of a playboy. Anyway, some of my cousins will be wearing jeans, if only to drive my great-grandma crazy. We all have a bone to pick with her and this is their way of rebelling, you know," she grinned at him.

"But not you?"

"I have the same bone to pick with her, no worries," she nodded. "However, I found out that wearing jeans at the dinner table would upset my mom as well so..." she shrugged. "Anyway, you look great and if Matt doesn't come in his business suit, you'll be one of the best dressed men at the table, so you have nothing to worry about," Becka patted his arm reassuringly.

Bryan nodded and pushed her toward the hallway so they could leave. When Becka saw all her fall and winter coats on the floor, she groaned. She hadn't realized what had happened when she stormed out earlier. He just grinned at her and patted her shoulder to show her it was not a problem for him.

"It's all right, Becka. At least now that I'm prepared to see things flying around, this isn't such a big shock to my system," he told her with the same grin on his lips.

She narrowed her eyes again. She was trying to discern whether he was making fun of her or not, but chose not to reply. She started picking the clothes up. Bryan helped her and they finished in no time, so they could finally leave.

***

Becka admired how he drove. Bryan was confident, but he wasn't aggressive. He didn't want to prove anything to anyone and he didn't care if others tried to overtake his car.

"Did you tell your parents you were bringing me to dinner?" he asked, glancing at her and taking in her posture.

She looked like a Madonna, all in white, with her hands folded neatly in her lap and serenity written all over her face.

She nodded, "I told them I'd come with my boyfriend but I didn't give them any details."

He glanced at her, surprised. In his book, women would give all the details, including the ones they shouldn't. That was something very new for him.

"Don't tell me they didn't ask any questions," he showed his scepticism to her words.

185

Becka fidgeted in her seat for a few seconds, but decided she'd better be open with him so she replied, "Well, all right. It seems you know already. Mom was very happy to hear I finally had a boyfriend, because she didn't think I'd ever get one. You know, I had that bad habit of chasing all the guys away… They were either too boring or too annoying, so… no big deal… Anyway, she asked just a minimum of questions and I gave her your name and a general description. That's all. Father wanted to know more, but I cut it short. He's overprotective and he can drive me crazy. Plus, he'd send my brother your way to make sure everything is all right for his little girl and that would be just too embarrassing."

Bryan laughed hearing her morose tone and glanced at her again just in time to see her pout. She had her moments when she resembled a teenager but he didn't mind that either, although until the moment he met her, he had never glanced at the teenagers that crossed his path.

"You wouldn't laugh if he'd sent Alex your way," she advised him. "Alex is a sweet brother, but he can be a pain in the butt all the same."

Bryan laughed harder. He had never imagined his sweet Becka would use such words and it was refreshing to see she could constantly surprise him. He wouldn't have enjoyed a linear relationship either.

CHAPTER TEN

Bryan felt stupid carrying his big bouquet of roses and waiting in front of Becka's parents' house.

Becka had insisted they could just go inside, but he had declined her proposition and told her to ring the bell as normal people would do when they went to visit someone. Becka mimicked a sign to show him she thought he was crazy, but seeing his steely determination, she gave in.

The woman rang the bell and waited anxiously next to him for the door to open. She wondered what her mother would say seeing her in front of the door since she had never rung the doorbell. Normally, she would just barge in.

Becka had been impressed when Bryan took a huge bouquet of roses from the back seat, after they stopped in front of her parents' house. She wouldn't have believed the tough guy would think of flowers.

Now, she was amused because she saw how uncomfortable he was standing there with those flowers in his hand. Truth be told, he didn't look like the type of guy who'd carry flowers. It was just not him. Suddenly, a thought crossed her mind and she frowned. She turned to him.

"You never brought me flowers," she accused him morosely.

At her unexpected outburst, Bryan turned his eyes to her and looked at her as if she had grown a horn right on her forehead. Her outburst had come out of nowhere.

For a moment, he didn't understand what had upset her and then, when the meaning sank in, with a puzzled frown between his eyebrows, he replied, "First of all, our dates have been a bit unconventional, baby. Coming to take you out for a sail or coming to apologize didn't seem to require flowers.... Okay, maybe when I came to apologize," he stopped for a second, reconsidering what he was saying.

Bryan suddenly realized that exactly when he came to apologize had been the moment when he should have brought her flowers, but that thought had never crossed his mind.

To cover his blunder, he continued in force, "Second, what flowers could I bring you when you have that garden? How could I compete with that?"

"It's not about competing, Bryan," she dismissed his excuse with a flutter of her hand. "Look at you. You bought flowers for my mother. My mother has a garden as well, so... the question remains. Why wouldn't you buy flowers for me?" she asked showing that stubborn streak of hers, although she was aware she had chosen a man who could show romance in other ways, but wouldn't bring flowers. It was just not his type and that was just her luck.

Bryan shook his head as if he'd needed to clear his mind and then he decided to answer. Exactly when he opened his mouth to reply, the door opened and a beautiful woman, in her fifties, smiled at them both, saving him from an answer that might have upset her even more.

He glanced at the woman framed in the door and noticed Becka was almost the exact replica of her mother. Bryan smiled and thought she would look great in her advanced age considering her heritage.

"Oh, sweetheart, you're finally here," the woman cooed and hugged Becka, kissing both her cheeks after the European fashion.

She squeezed the young woman a little more and then she finally turned to Bryan with sparkling eyes.

"Who do we have here, dear?" she asked.

Hearing her talk, Bryan was happy Becka hadn't inherited her mother's voice, too. It was one of those voices he couldn't stand. It reminded him of his mother's constant whining and recriminations. Yet, he continued smiling since he couldn't do otherwise. He knew he couldn't wince. He had to keep that phony smile on his lips although it required a real effort. Yet, wincing wouldn't have marked a very good beginning for his visit and it might have had long-term bad consequences.

He stretched his hand and said, "I'm Bryan, madam."

He shook her hand briefly and offered her the flowers, which were still a reason for discontent for Becka. He made a mental note to buy her flowers and as soon as possible.

Women loved flowers, he remembered, and associated romance with them, although he didn't understand why. He believed in showing what he felt through what he did. Bringing flowers didn't come too high on his list.

Becka's mother, Emilie, smiled at him in turn and invited both inside, constantly chattering and making him feel uncomfortable. Bryan was there for Becka, though, and he was decided to make every effort not to upset her or embarrass her in front of her family. If he had to listen to that woman's talking all evening, he would do that.

Becka's parents lived in a real mansion, given the size of the building. His house was big, according to his standards, but this one was much more than that. From outside, it was quite impressive and somehow intimidating, but then the inside of the house seemed much more imposing.

The size of the entrance hall was on the generous side and the floor sported tiles with a floral motive. Stunned, he noticed the left wall was lined with a beautiful table, which screamed that it had been made somewhere in the 18th century. It wasn't something he'd have chosen for his entrance hall. He was convinced that table had a place in a museum.

The hallway led to a circular room where he could see the same tiles but with a geometrical motive this time. That room seemed to be another hallway and that perplexed him. He couldn't understand the necessity of having two of them.

Once inside the circular room, he could hear several voices coming from somewhere on the left. The voices were mingling in chatter, but he couldn't make out any words. It was just a cacophony of gibberish.

Now, seeing her parents' house, Bryan was positive Becka never had any shrewd intentions on his wealth and her anger at the lake made more sense to him. His accusation must have come like a blow. He imagined she had felt hurt and insulted at the same time, and she had had all the right to feel that way.

He wasn't sure if he could compare what he possessed with her family's wealth. That was by far the house of a very rich family and he wondered how it was possible his Becka was living in that small house in town when her parents were living the way they did. It wasn't like they hadn't loved their daughter from what he had seen so far.

Bryan wasn't disappointed though, since he liked to think she was as unspoiled and real as she seemed. She didn't appear to be touched by the rich girl syndrome.

She wasn't demanding and she didn't ask for expensive clubs or restaurants and she had even enjoyed his cooking which, in his opinion, was nothing someone could find in the restaurants en vogue.

Emilie led them to the living room, which was at least ten times larger than Becka's. It was a vast space covered by several Aubusson carpets, but it still seemed to have difficulty containing all the people inside.

Bryan had the feeling he had walked into the middle of a big party. He had thought he would come only for a family dinner, though.

Looking around, he noticed some of the faces he'd seen in the pictures displayed in Becka's bedroom the night before.

Becka sensed he was uncomfortable and took his hand, giving it a little squeeze to encourage him. The man glanced at her and she could see the questions in his eyes and squeezed his hand again to let him know everything would be all right. She was wrong, though.

"I told you I have a big family, Bryan. At least, you can meet them all at once and that is done. I see everybody is here," she smiled at him and, as always, her smile had the power to make him relax.

A middle-aged man, almost of the same height as Bryan, came to them with supple steps and hugged Becka.

"How are you, sweetheart? We haven't heard much from you for the last two weeks, I think?" he phrased his reproach in a mild way.

"Oh, daddy, I'm fine. And I've talked to you, how can you say I haven't?" she replied and her voice showed her love for the man.

"I've said 'not too much', Becka, not that you haven't talked to us at all," he corrected her gently, then turned his eyes to Bryan.

Bryan noticed the older man's dislike immediately. It wasn't very difficult to spot it, as it was there in his eyes for everyone to see. He didn't want to let anything ruin Becka's day, so he tried hard not to show any expression on his face. Becka was a smart woman and she would have seen immediately something was amiss.

"So who do we have here?" Gabriel asked with a grave tone.

"Daddy, this is my boyfriend, Bryan," Becka chimed in, her happiness evident in her voice.

Bryan shook the older man's hand and lowered his head respectfully. He didn't know what to say to him and he didn't want to get into any argument if it was possible to avoid it.

However, Bryan was as wrong as Becka. No matter what he wanted, things had a way of evolving without asking for his opinion.

More people came around them and he began to feel crowded. Although everyone was kind to Becka, almost all of them were throwing him dirty looks as if he had come out right from the sewer. They seemed not to like her choice in boyfriends at all.

Bryan told himself he didn't care and that, in the end, they'd have to accept his presence in Becka's life. He didn't intend to let them chase him away.

Gabriel, Becka's father, decided he would be the first to begin the attack against him.

"So, what do you think you're doing with my little girl?"

"Daddy!" Becka gasped stunned by her father's outburst and turned to him with wide eyes and her little arched mouth opened in a perfect '*o*'.

"I beg your pardon?" Bryan inquired with a cool voice, although the question had angered him.

He had a pretty good idea he wasn't part of their social class, but that didn't mean he was nothing.

"You heard me very well, young man," Gabriel repeated. "What do you think you're doing with my girl? First of all, you're far too old for a girl like her," her father reiterated his bad feelings towards Bryan.

"Father, I think I can choose anyone I want," Becka started in a quarrelsome tone, but she couldn't go too far because she was interrupted immediately.

"Yes, sweetheart, you can, but choose someone of your own age," her father replied conciliatorily.

"And maybe not a felon, Becka, if that's possible. Look at his scar," Ariel chose to interfere, turning her nose up at the scar lining his cheek.

By now, Bryan's face looked as if it had been chiseled into stone. He had thought about this meeting and he had known that those would be their concerns, but now that everything was real, there, he felt chilled to the bone.

The man didn't like how things were going because it seemed his relationship with Becka was on the line.

He chose not to reply to Becka's sister, but he judged her in a second. She was one of those uptight women who had the misfortune to have had a bad hand dealt in life and took it out on everyone else.

"Becka knows what she's doing," her cousin Jay jumped into the melee and gained Bryan's gratitude. "You all know she's the smartest of us when it comes to people. And I wouldn't talk if I were you," he turned to Ariel.

Bryan liked that man. He was on his side and even though he knew Jay was a gambler, that didn't matter at all then. The important thing was he took Becka's side and tried to cut Ariel down a notch.

"How dare you?" Ariel started shouting. "How dare you to say something like that to me? She's my sister and I have to look out for her."

"Yes," Alex got involved in the general discussion.

Bryan knew he was Becka's brother because she had showed him his picture the night before.

"You should leave Ariel alone. And you Becka should think a little better about the kind of people you get involved with."

"I should? I should think a little better?" Becka's voice increased in intensity. "How dare you talk about Bryan like that, you moron? He's ten times better than you."

By now she was shouting and Bryan could see a few knick-knacks took off and swirled to the floor, followed by a few pillows that were on a sofa. Nobody cared, apparently. Probably such scenes were usual occurrence around there.

"Becka, baby," he touched her arm and tried to soothe her, but she wouldn't have it.

She turned to the mob with her hands fisted on her hips and said, "This is my boyfriend, and I emphasize, *my boyfriend*. Mark my words: either you start treating him as he deserves and welcome him into our family or I'm out of here."

Jay intervened immediately: "Don't worry, Becka, I have your back. I support you all the line. Hey, man," he said and stretched his hand to Bryan. "Hope you're fine. This is a crazy bunch, to be sure. You just don't pay any attention to them and everything will be just fine. Becka knows what she's doing," he repeated his earlier comment, tapping Bryan's shoulder.

Bryan shook his hand smiling. Beside Emilie, who might have just been playing the role of a good hostess, this was the first friendly face he had seen in that room.

His joy was short-lived though, when a very old woman with the whitest hair he had ever seen approached them with heavy steps. Everyone made way for her.

She seemed to be a very important part of the family. Everyone deferred to her. Bryan took in her stature and admired her posture.

She might have been old, but she walked like a general. The lines on her face showed she had

had tragedy in her life. She didn't seem a pleasant woman, but she was certainly formidable for such an old lady.

"So you're the fortune hunter, I see," she said in a booming voice, piercing him with her eyes.

For a moment, silence reigned in the room. Most of them had thought of that, but up to that moment, no one had dared to bring the subject up into the open. They looked to each other in shock, but aside from the raised eyebrows and a few open mouths, no one moved or said anything.

Becka and Bryan looked at her with stunned eyes and then looked at each other. The irony was lost on the others, but not on them. Both of them burst into laughter and Becka tumbled in his arms, laughing like a lunatic.

Everyone was staring at them, thinking they had gone mad. No one understood what was so humorous in accusing someone of being a gold digger.

Becka pulled back a little and looking at Bryan, asked him through guffaws of laughter, "How does it feel to be at the other end of the stick?"

Bryan laughed again and kissed her mouth soundly which drew a few gasps from the crowd around. Apparently, that was not sanctioned behavior in that house. The two of them didn't care though.

All the tension Bryan had felt before was gone now. Becka could have that effect on him. He wrapped an arm around her shoulders and the two of them faced the audience.

"Well, ma'am," he said politely, watching the old woman steadily, and bowing his head for a second, just as a belated sign of respect, "here I am. Not a fortune hunter, but I'm still here and I intend to stay. Not necessarily in this house," he thought to specify so no one misunderstood him, "but on Becka's side."

The old woman narrowed her eyes dangerously at him and said in a crisp voice, "I don't like him, Becka. Throw him back into the pond."

Becka stared at her great-grandma in shock and shook her head. She expected some opposition, but she didn't expect to hear things like that. Any sense of decorum had disappeared and everyone was attacking Bryan as if he had been a lowlife.

"He's not a fish to throw back in the pond and he's not an object," she said in a steely voice, Bryan had never heard before.

He thought that now he had the possibility to see another side of Becka and this side of hers was as fascinating as the others.

"He's a human being, a man, and he is mine, regardless if you like him or not. You don't decide for me. I love him and he loves me, and that's it. Case closed," she stated with determination, waving her hand and tapping her right foot for good measure.

A young man, close in age to him, came forward and stretched his hand to Bryan, "Welcome to the tribe, man, even if it's a loonie bin. I'm Matt. I think Becka chose well," he said in a serious tone.

Bryan shook his hand. The sincerity in Matt's voice impressed him. Finally, there was another one who welcomed him among them without taking shots at him first.

"Thank you, Matt," he said. "It's a pleasure to meet you. I can assure you of that," Bryan said smiling widely.

"Nonsense," the old bat retorted, taking a step forward. "Becka, end this stupid relationship right now. This is not the type of man with whom you should associate. If you do need someone, we'll find you a nice man from a good family."

Her voice carried far. She was the type of woman that expressed her opinions loudly and usually everyone listened to her. Not this time though.

Becka took his hand and said, "We're leaving, Bryan. If my family doesn't understand to accept you, then we'll go and that's it. I won't come to the next dinners, mother, I hope you understand," she said to her mother over her shoulder, heading to the door and pulling Bryan after her.

Emilie was in shock. She whimpered and covered her mouth with a trembling hand. She knew her Becka and her stubbornness. When she decided something, then nothing could make her change her mind and she didn't want to lose her youngest child.

"Becka, please," she pleaded, but Becka didn't give any sign she had heard her and continued her way to the door.

"If you leave this house now, with him, I'll have the fund trust changed on Monday morning. You will get nothing," her great-grandma said in a categorical voice. "He'll leave you then, because there'll be no money to feast on, but it would be too late for you to get your money because I won't change my decision."

Everyone froze. No one had ever thought Rebecca could do such a thing. She hadn't threatened Matt when he came with Velma or Jay when he tried to pull one over her. They knew when she made a decision about something, she didn't revisit her decision.

Becka stopped and turned back to her, pulling always Bryan in her wake. He could feel her shake with rage and was sure everything would start flying around in a moment.

Becka stopped before Rebecca and in a clipped tone replied, "I don't need your trust money. They come with strings attached, strings I don't like. You can take it and do whatever you want with."

"Hmm," the old bat replied looking at her sharply. "And how would you live? And what about this one?" she pointed to Bryan. "Do you think he'll still stay with you once you're penniless?" she said looking at Bryan with scorn.

"First of all, dear great-grandma," said Becka in a falsely sweet voice, "people work nowadays and they earn money to live on. Few need trust funds to pay for their daily expenses. I'm young and I can work. And if you're willing, we can make a bet Bryan won't leave me," she ended triumphantly and Bryan loved her even more in that moment.

"You think so, girl? Go ahead then, leave this house. Let's see who'll pay for your school and for your house and clothes and food. You think he'll keep you?" she tilted her head to Bryan with disdain.

"As a matter of fact, yes," he intervened in their argument for the first time. His voice was calm and businesslike. "I can afford to pay both for her school and for her house. She deserves it. Actually, she deserves much more and I intend to see that she gets everything she wants," he concluded.

Marjory came forward and spoke for the first time, "Grandma, you've done a lot of things to all of us along the years and no one has ever said anything. I think it's time for you to think of others, not only of what you want and how you think things should be because, I must tell you that, you're not always right. Becka is a smart girl, maybe smarter than many in this group," she said, looking around at the people surrounding them, and continued, "She found someone she loves and it's clear to me he loves her, too. I think you'd better let them be."

Gabriel looked at his wife and saw how desolate she was at the thought of losing her daughter. He didn't feel too comfortable with that either. Becka was the apple of his eye and he hadn't taken into consideration he would lose her because of his stubbornness.

He still thought Bryan was a little too old for her and he was concerned about his scar. That scar might have been an accident, he couldn't know for sure, but it also might have been the result of a life outside the law and that worried him a lot.

"Son," he addressed Bryan, "I see my daughter is determined to be with you and I know very well that I can't do a damn thing about it. She has to live her life as she wishes and probably make her own mistakes. I don't want to lose my youngest child so... I think I'd have to welcome you in my house," he said extending his hand to shake Bryan's.

Bryan shook his hand, understanding how hard it was for Gabriel to accept him. In a way, he admired the man for putting his daughter first and for pushing his feelings aside.

He wasn't a naïve man and he didn't believe the man took a liking at him all of a sudden. He knew he would always be a reason for discord in their family.

Emilie was so happy her husband had decided not to shun their daughter that she started crying in earnest now. She went and hugged Becka as if she had returned from a very long trip and she had been away for years. After she cried over her for a few moments, she also went and hugged Bryan, who was effectively shocked seeing such an expression of affection from her.

However, not everyone was happy. He could hear murmurs around them and see a few unfriendly faces. The old bitty, Rebecca, was watching everything with an evil eye.

The most unfriendly face, beside Rebecca's, was Ariel's. She didn't like how the story was evolving and she decided it was high time she had done something about it.

"Father, you can't accept that. Becka's a child and has no idea what she's doing. You have to make her see how wrong she is."

"And I say she does know what she's doing," Matt intervened. "Could you let your bitterness and jealousy aside for a moment, Ariel, and be happy for her? It's obvious she loves him and love is not something to trifle with," he admonished her.

"You can't know she loves him," she retorted. "Your gift is not refined, so you can't be sure of what she feels and if you tell me you do, then you're lying," she shouted pointing to him.

"I know how she feels and not because I've read her mind," Matt replied in a calm voice. "I haven't even tried to. But it's obvious. Doesn't anyone else see it?" he turned around to sweep the others with his eyes, because he didn't believe everyone was blind.

"What do you mean?" Adam, his grandfather, asked. "If you haven't read her mind, then you can't be sure she truly loves him. No one can. She might just want to rebel against the family, which is perfectly normal at her age," he added shaking his head.

"She was furious just now," Matt pointed out. "You could see her tremble with anger. Have any of you seen anything flying around? Have you?" he repeated more strongly, looking at each of them.

Everyone was astonished, including Becka. She hadn't even realized that, even though she had been extremely furious, nothing had happened. She had unconsciously controlled her gift. She was so happy that she had been capable of controlling her gift that she simply jumped, pumping her hand in the air, and shouting, "Yay me," and hugged Bryan, who was laughing, seeing her so carefree although he wasn't very sure why she was so happy and what Matt was talking about.

"I did it, Bryan, I did it!"

"Yes, baby, you did. You rock," he replied, still laughing and lifted her up and swirled around with her, kissing her soundly.

The others were watching them, unable to believe their eyes. Some of the people from the younger generation were jealous little Becka was the first one to beat the odds and get control over her powers. Jay and Matt were happy for her and simply watched the couple with wide smiles on their faces.

Once Bryan finally put her down, Matt hugged her, "You did it, little girl. More power to you," he said, kissing her cheek loudly.

Marjorie hugged Becka and turned to her grandmother, "Becka did her part. Now, you have to do yours. You have to give her the trust money. That's the right thing to do."

Rebecca smirked and replied, "In your dreams! She might love him and committed to him but he definitely doesn't love her. We'll have a meeting with the trustees and they will see what's what."

A few loud expressions of agreement were heard from the others who didn't like to be left behind by the youngest of the bunch.

Becka turned to Rebecca and told her, "I was serious when I said I didn't need your money, so the meeting with the trustees is unnecessary."

"Hmm, you're afraid of what they are going to say, I see. They'll see at once that he doesn't love you and you can't face the truth," Rebecca chuckled, satisfied to have been vindicated.

"No, it's not that. I'm not afraid because I know the truth and I don't need anyone's confirmation. I don't see the point in having Bryan paraded in front of them just to satisfy your sadistic pleasures," she replied.

"Baloney," Alex intervened with sarcasm. "If you don't want to meet with the trustees, it means you know he doesn't love you and you're afraid of what you'll hear."

"All right, everyone calm down," Bryan said with authority, when he saw that Becka was growing angrier.

He thought he had had enough of their drivel that evening and he wanted to end the discussion. "What are they talking about, sweetie?" he asked her.

"Really, it doesn't matter because I won't take her money," she answered with obstinacy.

"You don't need her money, Becka, and if you don't want it, then you won't take it, that's not an issue. But there's more to it than that, Becka. So, what is it?"

Becka looked down and didn't want to answer. She didn't know what to do, as a matter of fact. It wasn't she didn't trust his feelings and she wasn't afraid the two trustees would tell her Bryan didn't love her. However, she didn't know how Bryan would react to that meeting and she preferred not to find out.

"I'll tell him, sweetie," Matt put a soothing hand on Becka's arm. "So you understand better, great-grandma here," he said pointing to Rebecca, "thought it would be funny to get her revenge on her unfaithful husband by putting a curse on the following generations."

Rebecca gasped hearing his disrespectful tone, "I thought you loved me," she accused Matt.

Matt waved her concerns away, "I love you, that's not the issue here. It doesn't mean, though, I'm not upset being your Guinea pig, great-grandma," he told her and then turned to Bryan. "Anyway, Bryan, this is how things are. None of us can refine and control their powers until we fall in love for real and we commit to the person we love. Now, let me explain to you what's with the trust money. We can access the trust money only if the person we love also loves us in return and commits to us. And that's determined by a pair of trustees who are mind readers," Matt finished his explanation.

"Oh, I see," Bryan said nodding. "So, those trustees would be able to say if I love and commit to Becka, as well. That's the bone of contention here." He turned to Becka, "I understand you don't want her money and I agree with you. I don't want it, either. Is this the only reason you don't want to see the trustees, though?" he inquired.

"Well, not really… I don't know how you'd feel to have someone read your mind," she admitted.

"So it's not because you don't trust my love," he specified, staring into her eyes steadily.

"Of course not," she snapped at him.

"All right, then," he concluded and turned to Matt. "This mind reading, are there consequences to that?"

"Consequences?" Matt asked puzzled.

"Yes, you know like you could lose some of your mental capabilities or you might be persuaded to do something you don't want to…," Bryan specified.

"Oh, that," Matt dismissed his concerns, "no, nothing like that, don't worry. The only downside to it is that they can see what you think."

"Well, if they're not concerned I might swear at them, I don't mind," he said turning to Becka. "Sweetie, I know you don't want the money and I strongly advise you not to accept it. I have enough for both of us and we won't starve or have to cut down on too many things. However, if this will bring peace of mind to your parents, I'm willing to do it, all right?"

Everyone stared at him with disbelief. For a few moments, no one was able to do or say anything.

Only Becka hugged him and whispered, "For them, it would be great. But you don't have to do it if you don't want to. I trust you, and that's what is the most important."

"I know, baby," he whispered back. "But if we can make them feel at ease, why not?"

Becka nodded and hugged him with more force. She couldn't believe he would do something like that for her and he loved him more for his thoughtfulness.

"You think you can play them?" Ariel asked with contempt. "Jay tried and it didn't work, so you won't be able to, either," she told him.

Bryan looked at her like she had lost her mind for a moment, but then his eyes simply swept over her as if he had dismissed her, which made her angrier and she left the room furiously.

"Why don't we invite the trustees here, now?" Rebecca asked sweetly. "There's no better time than the present. They're two of my dearest friends and they won't refuse me... I don't want to wait until Monday and hear something happened and you couldn't make it to the meeting," she addressed to Bryan.

"That's just fine with me," he replied to her. "Invite them over. Maybe we can have a drink while we wait," he told Emilie. "My throat is a little dry after so much talking."

He was aware he might have come across as being rude, but he did need a glass of something strong. There mightn't have been any kind of witchy things going on but he felt a little tired after all that commotion.

"I'll bring you a scotch," Matt said. "I'll take one for me as well. I do need one after this ruckus," he continued and left for the table where several bottles of alcohol were kept.

Becka took Bryan's hand and pulled him to a love seat. She didn't intend to let anyone come close to him after they'd behaved so horribly with him. They sat down, and Bryan stroked her arm to soothe her.

"It'll be over soon, love, and then we can go home," he said.

"Where's home, Bryan?" she asked him with wide eyes.

He took a moment to think, but there wasn't much to think over. He knew he needed her all the time and even though their relationship was so young, he didn't need time to see where it was going because he didn't intend to let her go.

"It's up to you," he answered. "I know what I want and that's being with you. Now, if you want to wait and see how it'll be, we can wait for a while and see each other every day. If you feel the same, then we can choose to live together, either in your house or in mine. Of course, mine is there on that island and it means we have to sail every day to town if you need to be in town…"

Becka squeezed his hand and replied, "I'd say wherever you want is fine with me, but I'd lie."

Bryan froze hearing her answer. He couldn't believe his ears. His hopes were crushed and his expression steeled once more.

"I knew you wouldn't continue with this charade, Becka," Ariel said with glee.

They had been so focused on each other they hadn't heard her sneaking up on them. Hearing her voice, they looked up at her. Her face shined with delight and she was looking at Bryan with triumph in her eyes.

"What's going on?" Matt asked returning with the drinks.

"Not much," Bryan muttered. "Probably, I'll have to go now," he said and tried to stand up, but Becka pulled him back next to her.

"What are you talking about? Why would you leave?" she asked him and her eyes were stricken with pain.

"You said that…" Bryan started to say and she interrupted him.

"I said I preferred to live in town. You know I don't like waking up early in the morning and coming all the way from your island to town in the morning would be awful. Of course, we can spend our weekends there. It is a wonderful place but I don't see myself living there permanently. That's what I said."

"No, it isn't," Ariel snapped. "You were very clear you didn't want to live with him," she pointed out.

"No, I wasn't. I might not have phrased my thoughts correctly, but what I meant was that I wanted to live in town so you should stop being so delighted," Becka snapped back at her.

Ariel put her hands on her hips and repeated stubbornly, "No, Becka, you said that…"

"Shut up for a second," Bryan barked at her and she stopped, too stunned by his rudeness to say anything anymore. "Now, Becka, let's clarify. Do you want me to live with you in your house?"

"Yes, of course, that's what I want. And you said I could choose," she replied stubbornly.

"Yes, you can choose, that's not the issue here. As long as you don't ask me to leave from your life, I'll agree to everything," he said, taking her hand with tenderness.

The icy block that had begun to form inside him started to melt. He was relieved he hadn't been wrong about her.

Becka hugged him and kissing his lips, she whispered, "Don't be stupid. How can I want you to leave when I can't function without you?"

Happy, Bryan hugged her tight and kissed her hair in relief. He didn't notice Ariel left in a huff and he didn't actually care what she was doing. After holding Becka tightly to him for a while, he let her go with regret and took the glass from Matt's hand.

"You don't know how much I need this now, man," he said to Matt.

"I can imagine," he mused. "You do look like a man in need of something strong, indeed."

Bryan took his glass and swallowed half of the whiskey at once, feeling less tense afterwards.

He tapped Matt's shoulder saying, "Thanks, man. Good stuff, by the way."

"Yes, Uncle Gabriel always has good stuff handy. He's the most generous of the uncles," Matt said, elbowing Bryan, "Keep that in mind. If you go visit Uncle Michael, you're out of luck. He doesn't take out the good stuff for guests. It's just for him."

Bryan laughed and felt included in the inside stuff. Matt was indeed the good man Becka had described. Bryan thought Matt would make a good friend besides being one of his few allies in that house.

They chattered for a while, most of the time with Becka next to him, hanging on his arm, but some of the time she took off to talk to her cousins or aunts.

Matt was amused seeing Bryan, who looked quite impressive, as he was so tall and fit, looking around, so lost, trying to find Becka in the sea of people crowding his aunt's living room.

When the two trustees arrived, which didn't surprise anyone, as all of them knew Rebecca's reputation, the chatter stopped and the family's glances shifted between Becka and Bryan to the trustees. All of them were impatient to hear the verdict.

Yet, Bryan started to sweat. A thought had crossed his mind some time earlier and was still nudging at him. He had wondered if the old bitty had the trustees in her pocket because, in that case, they would say what she wanted to hear and he was convinced Becka would believe them.

They were witches after all and they could read minds. His word against theirs might mean close to nothing.

Gabriel came with the two trustees to introduce them to Bryan. "This is Mr. Thompson and this is Mr. Jones."

Bryan shook their hands and expected to see what they had to say. Becka had come next to him and slipped her arm around him as if she had wanted to comfort him. He wrapped his arm around her shoulders as well and looked inquiringly at the two old men.

No one was talking anymore. Bryan glanced around and saw expectation on everybody's faces. Only Rebecca didn't show any. Her face was expressionless, even though she was trying to stare him down with her eyes.

Bryan shrugged and turned to the two men to see what they wanted from him. Once his attention was on them again, he felt a light probing in his mind and frowned.

"He can feel it," Mr. Jones whispered to Mr. Thompson. "Did you see?"

"Yes, I see he does," he replied. "Well," he said turning towards Rebecca, "You know I won't lie, Rebecca. I know what you want me to say, but the truth is he does love her and he's committed to this relationship."

Mr. Jones approved as well with a nod and Rebecca frowned. Everyone was waiting to see what she was going to do and they didn't have to wait for too long.

"Very well, Becka and Bryan," she said, "if this is the case, then you have my congratulations. I won't lie and say I like you," she said to Bryan squarely, "however, I'll welcome you to the family for as long as you're faithful to Becka."

Bryan nodded. He understood her feelings even though he didn't agree with her. He imagined it wasn't so easy to accept the fact that a man like him would date a young woman like Becka.

"On Monday morning, come to my office and I will make the transfer of your funds," Mr. Thompson addressed to Becka.

Bryan intervened right away, remembering her stubborn refusal of the money, "Do you want that money, Becka? Because I do have enough for both of us."

Becka took a moment to think. Finally, she shook her head, "No, I don't. I didn't like what happened here tonight because of that fund and I don't want to have anything to do with it."

"Oh, my God, are you stupid?" Ariel shouted. "How can you reject so much money? Didn't you want to open that stupid shop?"

"Calm down," Matt admonished her. "Becka, I understand your feelings in this matter, but the money is yours and you should take it."

Becka shook her head and Bryan gathered her to him.

"If Becka wants a shop, I'll take care of that," he said. "I think we can skip dinner tonight, Becka, what do you say?"

She nodded and said, "Mom, dad, we're leaving now and we'll talk later, all right?"

Emilie teared up again when she hugged her daughter. She was happy Becka had found her love, but she was also sad her little daughter wasn't so little anymore. She hugged Bryan as well for good measure and he hugged her back with stoicism, although he wasn't very big on such gestures.

EPILOGUE

Eleven months later

"Gabriel, you have to come now. Now, I said," Bryan yelled into the phone.

"What the hell happened to you that you're in such a state?" Gabriel's voice boomed at the other end of the line.

"She's mad, that's what happened. She's lost her mind," Bryan yelled again.

"What are you talking about? What's going on there?" Gabriel snapped worried for his little daughter.

"She lied to me, you hear me? She lied and now, I don't know what to do," Bryan shouted.

"Okay, calm down, son, and tell me what the problem is. What could she have done to make you lose your calm like this?"

"She's giving birth now!"

"What do you mean *now*?" his father-in-law asked, scared witless.

"She didn't say anything all day and just now she told me she's ready. I asked her to go to the hospital and she said it wasn't time. That she planned it that way. She told me to call Marjorie, but no one's answering the phone at their place and I don't know what to do. I've never assisted in a birth. I haven't even watched a birth in a movie. Damn it! I've always walked away when there was a scene like that. What the hell am I going to do?" he lost his temper completely.

"Okay, okay, let's see. Calm down first! Marjorie is here. We'll come at once. I'll have her call you from the car so she can assist you by phone if… if… You know…" Gabriel ended in a weak voice.

"No, I don't know. I don't want to know. It's Becka we're talking about and I don't know anything."

A few murmurs came to him through the phone line. Gabriel was talking to someone.

"All right, Bryan, Marjorie said to calm down and she'll call you from the car."

"But…"

"No buts, man, just wait," Gabriel replied and hung up, leaving Bryan in silence.

***

"A girl and a boy, Bryan," Marjorie said. "Congrats to both of you. And you've done a good job helping Becka to bring the boy into the world. Have you thought of any names yet?"

Becka nodded exhausted and Bryan stroked her forehead lovingly. He turned to Marjorie and told her with pride, "He's Sean and our daughter is Lea." He looked at his wife again with love and kissed her, "You have to rest, baby."

217

She nodded and closed her eyes. The little
ones were sleeping soundly, as well, but Bryan
felt like he had climbed the Everest.

Author's Bio:

Rowena Dawn writes romance, reads thrillers and watches comedies. She likes walking through the woods but insanely loves the sea. She has a love - hate relationship with her writing and drives her dog crazy whenever she doesn't stop writing to take him out. And yes, she bakes, bread and cakes. Apparently good ones - they're always in demand.

Look for the second book in the series: "Matt's Dilemma" – it will come out soon

Other books by Rowena Dawn

Leap of Faith
Double-Edged – Book One in the Perfect Halves Series
Eyes in the Dark – Book Two in the Perfect Halves Series
Pulled In – Book Three in the Perfect Halves Series
Mr. (Almost) Right

Thank you for taking the time to read *Becka's Awakening,* the first book in the series **The Winstons**.

If you enjoyed it, please consider telling your friends or posting a short review.

Word of mouth is an author's best friend and much appreciated. Thank you,

Rowena Dawn